DESTROYED BY THE EVENTS OF THE DAY

CHAPTER 1

IT WAS A RUSE.

At 10:12 a.m., Michael Cloughey sat in a deep chocolate brown high-back leather office chair. Its wooden legs and bronzed appointments accented the baroque-style desk across from it as well as the wheat color of the walls. The rug under his feet was a burgundy low-nap, industrial-variety carpet. The color reminded him of red wine after it had been spat into a bucket at a wine tasting. The desk was supposed to provide the room with the look akin to a Victorian library; however, it actually gave the appearance that the room was being swallowed by an unhealthy and poorly maintained mouth right before a proper and long overdue cleaning. The chair's intention was to provide a semblance of professionalism, class, and taste. One might have even gone so far as to view it as a comfortable and warm place for a visitor to sit so they could express great, elaborate, and deep thoughts. To sink into a chair of such richness would inspire great clarity and envelop its resident in an embrace that only a king could bestow upon a servant. Certainly, a chair of such import had seen its share of vision, enlightenment, theatrical gesture, and engaged use. Certainly, the men and women who graced this chair with their rather pleasing and, at other times displeasing, derrieres were men and women who conquered worlds, rainmakers who challenged the status quo and provided the universe with breathtaking stances on important social issues and groundbreaking policies. Certainly, this chair was just making a brief stop in this room before eventually attending to the needs of a diplomat, a dignitary, a theologian, or a professor of applied engineering at the Massachusetts Institute of Technology.

It was all a ruse.

At 10:23 a.m., Michael Cloughey looked at the cream-colored face of the watch he wore on his right wrist and then slowly looked at his pant leg, adjusting it to align the delicately pressed crease with the front of his knee and down his shin. This would allow the folded cuff at the bottom to meet perfectly with the top of his shoe to form a fold that he deemed satisfactory. This, he hoped, would happen when he would finally have the opportunity to stand up and walk out of the room. Michael Cloughey saw no need for dress pants that were not creased or cuffed at the bottom. Pleats had not been a "thing" since the 1990s, but a full crease down the front of the pant leg was a standard and he would not entertain debate regarding this item. A fitted dress shirt pressed but not starched, with a tapered tie and tie clip led to a belt that matched the shoes, which led to the aforementioned creased pants that ended just touching the laced portion of a richly colored dress shoe, either a wing tip or cap toe. The tie always stopped at the end of the shirt where it met the belt. There were days Michael went through three or four attempts at making this happen with a tight Windsor knot. This morning it took him five and cost him almost twelve minutes. Today the brown leather Citizen watchband matched the brown leather belt that matched the brown leather of the shoes. As Michael left the house that morning at 6:40 a.m., he also made sure to swap the black leather briefcase he used the day prior for his fabric messenger bag with brown accents at the enclosure buckles and handle. This was coordination. It felt like order. It made him feel complete, confident.

At 10:24 a.m., the man behind the desk hung up his office phone and propped the same arm up under his chin with his first two fingers and thumb. This cradled his head in his palm, and the entire structure was then held up by an elbow that became rooted to the aforementioned too-large desk. Ironically, the elbow rested on a piece of paper that Michael noticed had the words "to do" written unconvincingly on them.

The man sighed.

———◆———

THIRTY-ONE YEARS AGO, WHEN HE WAS ELEVEN, Michael Cloughey was in a fistfight with another boy. Although the young man was both three years older and approximately a foot and a half taller, it did not stop Michael from defending the honor of a young childhood friend of his. Lara's name had been placed in the same sentence as the word "pig." When the fourteen-year-old refused to take it back and apologize, Cloughey slowly walked up to him and spit in his face. While the older boy was distracted, Cloughey punched him in the gut to chop him down to a more reasonable size. When the older boy fell to his knees to grab his stomach and gasp for the air that was just punched out of him, Cloughey punched him repeatedly in the face with both hands.

The older boy would arrive at the emergency room with a face that resembled a mix between an open pomegranate and a horribly tenderized steak. After a resetting of his nose and a combined twelve stitches to his lip and cheekbone, the older boy would have problems breathing through his nose for the rest of his life. This caused an incurable snoring habit that would eventually create a more intense sleeping problem, or rather a lack of sleep. Michael would know the most immediate and long-term effects of his brutality years later because the fourteen-year-old was his older brother, Sean.

Although this was a singular event of its kind that summer, it would not be an isolated event in Michael's life. Lara, the childhood friend who was defended that day, would grow up, and seventeen years later, she and Michael would marry. Sean Cloughey would preside over the overtly Catholic ceremony as the priest and pastor of St. Sebastian Parish. As he articulately and solemnly performed his duties as the Hand of the Holy Spirit in wedding Michael to Lara, Michael could still see a scar on the right cheekbone of Father Cloughey. He had never apologized to his brother for the events of that day so many years ago. It was not the first time that Michael had used his fists, his wrath, his rage, his spit, and his hate-filled words on another human being.

It, without question, would not be the last.

DESTROYED
BY THE EVENTS OF THE DAY

JOHN INFORTUNIO

Charleston, SC
www.PalmettoPublishing.com

Destroyed by the Events of the Day

First Edition
Author Photo by Connor Weitz

Hardcover ISBN: 978-1-68515-729-6
Paperback ISBN: 978-1-68515-730-2
eBook ISBN: 978-1-68515-731-9

For my parents, Marie and John Infortunio,
who instilled in me a love of literature,
and for my son, Kevin, my greatest achievement

CHAPTER 2

Michael Cloughey was born a twin. He would be told by his parents that his twin, John, lived for approximately one week and then died due to developmental complications. John would never be brought home. He would never share a room with Michael. He would never wear the infant clothing his parents had bought. He would never suffer an older brother's juvenile torment. John Jrs ashes would be buried in a small, disconsolate cemetery for deceased infants on the northern end of Long Island, New York. His almost nonexistent tombstone would read, "Baby Cloughey."

At a young age, Michael realized that he hated this conversation, the "dead twin brother" topic, the feeling one feels when they can do nothing and are not quite sure how to feel about not doing anything. He felt it was equally about the disappointment regarding his survival as it was about the infinite sadness associated with losing a child. It was tiring, and it became more exhausting the older he became. Michael knew where his brother had been buried; he stored away the notice of burial addressed to his parents. The cream-colored stationery with the St. Damascus Cemetery letterhead sitting at the top had been created by someone who was not a very proficient typist. He could tell by the lettering. Every so often, and more often as he read down the page, some letters appeared darker, and some appeared almost nonexistent for no explicable reason. An advanced typist was smooth and very uniform with their keystrokes. The letters and thoughts poured from their fingers onto the page, and the thoughts and appearance of the text were orderly and purposeful.

It frustrated Michael that his parents had had to read this letter informing them as to where John Jr. was buried, but it also irked him that they had had to absorb this news from such a poorly crafted document. The letter stated, "We sympathize with you on the death of your baby, but I am sure it will be of some consolation for you to know that the child is interred in a Catholic cemetery." It wasn't.

Although his parents had raised a healthy older son in Sean, Michael would be raised as if he were an only child. His mother, a schoolteacher, was doting and extremely affectionate, unfairly so. His father was an extremely quiet man who displayed his love through work and provisions. He said very little and never laid a hand, in either affection or punishment, on Sean or Michael. It was this untapped silence and consistently present uncertainty that Michael feared for the entirety of his father's life.

John Cloughey Sr. worked on Wall Street for over thirty years. He was not one of those men who spent the entire day screaming and shouting out trading orders and purchase prices. He did not spend his afternoons drinking his lunch nor his ten-minute breaks smoking five cigarettes. He was not a man who sought out the weakest newcomer to the floor to fuck him out of his daily trading allowance. He was an organizer, the man who sat behind the desk to handle the heaping piles of paperwork and dollar values all these trades equaled. Cloughey Sr. was an individual who kept one hundred moving parts together, and he used numbers to do it. Numbers did not lie; they did not exaggerate, and they did not tell sordid tales of greatness. They were what they were, and after all was done, all you had left was what was told to you in and by a number.

The greatness of a hitter in baseball is based upon a batting average, and a great pitcher is judged by their overall record and earned run average. Boston Red Sox outfielder Ted Williams had a career total of 7,706 at bats, and out of those at bats, he got 2,654 hits for a total lifetime batting average of .344. To this day, a .300 plus batting average is the litmus test for the overall success of a hitter. A season average of .300 or better is considered a highly successful season. The .300 number often determines which hitters are welcomed into the Hall of Fame. To John, that was all that need be known. The numerical value was the story, the absolute. Nothing about that could be a fallacy, an untruth. It could not be disproven, and it could not be denied. Numbers were the fundamental existentialism, and he felt proud to realize their true value as that. Sure, the subjectivity of art and music had their place, and he had no idea what kind of human being Ted Williams was, but there was no mistaking the unmistakable fact that the universe could be measured, determined, and understood and numbers were the driving force. So, for John Cloughey Sr., answers to questions about when to split a stock, when to get more aggressive with an investment, and when was it a good time to pull away from small-cap stocks for a large yield were simple. The difficult life questions, for him, were found in what you say to your son when he says, "I love you, Dad."

Michael and Sean's father was a man of quiet and methodical habit, a fundamentalist, not of the religious Bible-thumping variety but rather of industrialism, fortitude, and self-minimalism. John Sr. would wake up every day at five o'clock in the morning, get dressed, work until five o'clock in the evening, arrive home, eat dinner, prepare for the next morning, and go to bed at nine o'clock. Save for the occasional, carefully placed brief break, his routine failed him not. From his father Michael learned two valuable ideals that he would attach to his id, ego, and superego. The first was that hard work and order were the great equalizers. Hard work leveled the playing field. One evening while walking his son to the candy store, John Sr. told Michael that no matter how much talent, skill, or God-given ability a man has, he could always be beaten, even crushed by the hard work of another man. God gave only certain people the gift of hard work. Michael did not know why his father had chosen to tell his ten-year-old son this careful detail. He was sure he never told it to Sean, and this made him love his father and this information even more. The second thing Michael learned from his father was how to appreciate things, anything. If it was worth holding onto for just a minute, you should appreciate it for as long as you had it. A man who was raised during the height of the Great Depression not only understood this feature of existence but lived it as if it were the eleventh commandment. When Michael graduated from college, his father gave him an Elgin wristwatch. The card attached to the gift read, "Mike, appreciate every second. Your Father."

John Cloughey Sr. was fifteen years older than his wife. He was always older than the fathers of Michael's friends. He was always older than the fathers of Michael's girlfriends. This was not something that escaped Michael and Sean's notice. When Michael looked at his father, he always felt a profound amount of respect and gratitude for what his father provided his family with. He was grateful for the toys, the trips to baseball games, the candy, the new baseball glove, and the bike. Although he was not crushed by it, the words "I love you, Mike" would have been a fine birthday gift—even if it was just once, even if it was not meant. It was impossible for Michael, or any kid his age, to realize at the time that his parents had provided both Sean and he with a very comfortable middle-class upbringing, and with it came the ideals of Catholicism.

Catholicism to the Cloughey family was a safety net, the belt with the suspenders. They were not the type of people to sit around and contemplate theology and belief and faith. They were not "preachy." Their friends did not have to be Catholic. Honestly, they disliked Catholics. They went to mass because it was what you did on Sunday mornings. It made your coffee and pancakes easier to digest. John Sr. often used the actual mass as a time to mentally wander off and betray his prideful focus. He never responded to recited psalms. He never outwardly said an Our Father. He never even received Communion. He randomly gave at collection when the long-handled wicker baskets were placed in front of parishioners' faces in such a quick and sweeping gesture that they seemed to be levitating. He sometimes even let Michael or Sean drop the change into the basket if they asked politely on their way to mass. John Sr. stood, sat, and kneeled at the appropriate moments. It was as if the mass itself was a time-out away from Wall Street, nagging voices, obligations. He felt safe there, secure. One of the only things Michael and Sean ever truly agreed upon and at later times laughed about was that they were both strongly convinced their father learned how to sleep with his eyes open during mass. The nine o'clock Sunday mass was usually said by Father Delaguarda. He was one of the oldest priests at St. Sebastian Parish and the only Italian priest. He was the favorite of John Sr. because his homilies were usually over twenty minutes long, making the mass close to one hour in length overall. When he was much older and held hostage by Alzheimer's disease, John Sr. confided to Michael, in a moment of frustrating clarity perhaps, that he only went to a Father Delaguarda mass because it was longer and gave him more time to "get away" during church. Michael was not exactly sure what his father was hinting at, but he ended his confession with "Boy, that guy loved the sound of his own voice."

CHAPTER 3

IT WAS NO SURPRISE TO ANYONE IN THE CLOUGHEY household when Sean applied to be and was quickly chosen to be an altar boy. Sean was a lectern. Sean worked in the St. Sebastian Rectory answering the phones and ordering Communion wafers. Sean sold mass cards to women who were still mourning the deaths of their husbands twenty years after their husbands had left this mortal world. Sean even volunteered to work midnight mass on Christmas Eve to help with the collection on the busiest night of the year. This infuriated Michael because he was under the strong belief that this delayed the arrival of Santa Claus. One year Michael asked Santa, during a highly focused face-to-face meet and greet on the seventh floor of Macy's department store on Fulton Street, Brooklyn, for an Ives 1122 O gauge electric train set that he had coveted for over a year. When he awoke on Christmas morning, he was met with a football, two Tonka trucks, and a harmonica.

Michael openly blamed Sean for this and told his parents that Sean was in cahoots with Jesus and Santa to fuck him out of his train set. Michael was eight and a half years old. While Sean truthfully never enjoyed the wait in full winter regalia in the sweltering department store, he went because they were always treated to lunch at Junior's right afterward. That lunch always ended with strawberry cheesecake. Enduring a ninety-degree sweatbox wearing four layers was worth any event that ended with an enormous slice of Junior's cheesecake.

So years later when Sean sat down and explained to his family that he was entering the seminary, it should not have been a surprise to John Sr. and his wife. Every parent believes their child will get married, have children, and provide grandchildren to them as a reward for the years of love and careful upbringing. Every parent harbors a deep desire to have a grandchild named after them as a tribute and homage to their parental greatness and superiority. Every parent wants to see their child hand them a baby and admit that they hope they can do as good a job as they did. It is an expectation. Sean and Michael Cloughey's parents were no different. When your oldest and most attractive son tells you he has been chosen by God to "report for duty," you either embrace it and thank God for the house call or you throw something fragile, fall to the ground, scream something indecipherable, and cry for about as long as it takes for Father Delaguarda to spit out a homily. Virginia Cloughey did the latter. John Cloughey Sr. looked at Sean straight in the eye while holding both of his shoulders in his hands at full arm's length. He nodded, got up, and went for a walk. He returned fifty-two minutes later with a newspaper that was rolled up so tightly it could have been used as a murder weapon.

What a young and highly aware Michael Cloughey knew that no one else in the Cloughey family guessed or perhaps even suspected was that Sean was a homosexual. Michael gathered some clues and made some unsuspecting observances during his teen years when he had begun the dating process. After finding all other girls aside from Lara Louise Trammell annoying, disgusting, and slightly repulsive. Michael began a rather successful and quite energetic dating career, leaving many of the formerly "yucky" girls in heaped masses crying because he wanted nothing to do with them after they allowed him to convince them they were spectacular and thus giving up their virginity to him in various places of public interest: parks, movie theaters, beaches, elevators, trains, arcades, pool halls, a chemistry laboratory, and even a fitting room at Macy's—he somehow felt that was fitting payback for the Christmas "snub" from Santa regarding his train set years earlier.

Michael Cloughey's early dating career was a thing of urban legend, myth, and public restroom stall poetry. He courted many, lied to most, and fucked almost all of them with the vigor and enthusiasm of a young, handshaking, baby-kissing politician running for state senator. He had a new line for each one and no truth for a single one of them. The faster they gave up their treasure to him, the quicker he became disinterested in even sitting next to them on the bus. He sought them out, and he hunted well. Hemingway would have wept at his abilities as a hunter and a lover.

There was one girl, Josephine, who had just moved into town two weeks prior to a famed Michael Cloughey breakup. She apparently had not heard of *the* Michael Cloughey, and she went so far as to make Michael look her in the eye as he promised her, she was *his* first sexual encounter as well. He did.

When it was over, he walked her home, and on her front porch, they bumped into her younger cousin, Audrey, whom Michael had told the same thing to the prior weekend. This brief, albeit awkward, encounter left Michael with a gash on his head and a broken knuckle on his right hand. When Audrey Peterson found out about Michael's addiction to girls' innocence like hers and Josephine's, she immediately went inside and roused the Peterson brothers, Thomas, and Dave. Michael put Tom in the hospital with a concussion after hitting him with a tree branch, and he nearly blinded Dave after punching him so hard that he fractured Dave's eye socket.

When Michael arrived home that night, he passed his brother's room to clean up, and he overheard his brother mumbling a prayer through the half-open door. It was at that very moment, at the young age of sixteen, that he knew his brother was a homosexual. He had never seen him with a girl. He had never even had a conversation with him about a girl. He had never shared the little jokes or glances at a secretly stowed away *Playboy* magazine that he was sure so many brothers did throughout their adolescence. Here he was on a Friday night in the middle of a particularly hot July, collecting the "essence" of every teenage girl he could capture, fighting off their brothers and breaking his hand in the process to come home and find his older brother on his knees praying to God. This was beyond a devotion and a dedication to an almighty, unseen deity. This was beyond a feeling of obligation to a creator. This was certainly beyond a weekend hobby for an Irish kid whose parents attended mass simply due to superstition. No, this was something other than repentance for his kid brother's sins. This was guilt. Michael never felt it, but he could identify it in a well-constructed lineup of other emotions that escaped him, such as pity, compassion, and sympathy. Guilt of what or from what he did not know. Sean never seemed to be the kind of kid who did anything worthy of guilt. Adolescent pranks were one thing, but Sean was praying as if the steak dinner had been served and the electric chair was waiting in the adjoining room.

Michael stepped into his brother's room that night, and he asked him what it was he felt so guilty about that he would be tormenting his young self on a Friday night alone in his room, praying. Michael's curiosity was genuine. His words were soft spoken and legitimately unwavering in their delivery considering the "conversation" he had just had with the Peterson brothers. Sean picked up his head and swept his thick black hair to the side of his face. He looked at his brother, his green eyes tired and long, and said, "Guilt is a feeling I really know, Mike. You should investigate it." When he noticed Michael's swollen hand, his eyes met Michael's and he asked, "How many?"

"Two."

He nodded.

He didn't ask Michael if he won the fight or even why he had fought.

He didn't have to.

He never had to.

CHAPTER 4

Virginia Cloughey's maiden name was LaPietra.
John Sr. called her Ginny, Sean called her Mom, and Michael
called her Yah. As a child, Michael tried to pronounce his
mother's name and he never could quite reach every syllable.
No matter how much John Sr. attempted to get him to pronounce his mother's name correctly, it would never stick. Even
at a young age Sean tried to get him to say "Mom," but Michael
would return the request with a harsh and threatening "Yah!"
So from the age of approximately two, it was Yah.

"Yah, can I have something to eat?"

"Yah, Sean took my baseball cards."

"Yah, this is Lara. Lara this is my mother, Virginia Francis
Cloughey."

Virginia filled the Cloughey household with love. Virginia
closed the distance of John's coldness with doting. Virginia
turned what would have been an emotionally empty house

into a home filled with humor, singing, smiling, and, above all, amazing food. For every disappointment her sons met, there was an appetizer. For every fight, there was an entrée, and for every failure, there was a dessert.

The morning after Michael's fight with the Peterson brothers, Yah made one of the biggest breakfasts Michael had ever seen. With his father working in the yard and Sean still sleeping, Michael sat down to a morning filled with eggs, pancakes, bacon, homemade biscotti, and fresh juice. Yah sat down with Michael and said nothing. She was mysterious and somewhat sad. Michael was scared, and he approached this woman differently than he always approached the woman who filled his home with laughter and lightness. With his body aching from the night before, Michael was not prepared for this type of breakfast.

His mother asked him what he would do if she wasn't with him and Sean. Michael didn't respond. He ate the breakfast. His mother asked him what he thought Sean would do if he had to live with their father alone. Michael didn't respond. He drank the juice. Yah asked Michael if he had ever heard of something called cancer.

He stopped eating. He said nothing. He felt dizzy and sick. His stomach felt tight, and his bowels felt like they were about to give way. He had heard of the thing she mentioned, and he knew it was not something he wanted to discuss, particularly not over a regal breakfast such as this, not on a morning like this. Michael looked at his mother and took a phony sip of his juice. He pushed his plate away. He stood up and crossed the table to where she sat, and he hugged her.

She placed her arm on his forearm, and she whispered, "I love you, Mikey."

"Thanks for the breakfast, Yah." That was as good as five *I love yous*. From his father, Michael Cloughey learned how to appreciate what he had and how to work hard enough to get what he didn't have. From his mother, Michael Cloughey learned how to love. It was she who instilled in her son the ability to love Lara, and it was this breakfast that would make Michael unable to even look at food the moment he ever felt nervousness, anxiety, or fear.

CHAPTER 5

THE MAN SITTING ACROSS FROM MICHAEL CLOUGHEY who had just hung up the phone was Ralph DiNardi. He was Michael's boss, the principal of the high school Michael taught at, and the owner of the impressive chair Michael found himself in. DiNardi was a man of curious motivations. He was personable, and he had a charisma that Michael and his colleagues had varied opinions on. Some liked this man and felt he was the individual to improve curriculum and develop teachers. Some thought he was a means to an end. Some, like Michael, felt he was a pseudo-intellectual incapable of original thought and vision. On one occasion when Michael proposed an idea regarding student evaluation through curriculum enhancement, he looked at Michael and said, "That sounds like a good idea. I'm not an idea guy." He used the first two fingers on each hand to symbolically bookend the word "idea" between.

Michael knew he was not an idea guy. He knew he was not a man capable of real thought. He could calculate numbers for budgetary purposes. He was able to shake the hands of unassuming parents while failing them and their children. He was able to look at people and sigh to express his dismay and disappointment all while holding a dark secret.

He was as phony as his chair.

Ralph DiNardi had no ideas. He had no vision. He had no clue as to how to stand in front of a room and educate the students Michael faced on a daily basis. Everything DiNardi learned came from a manual, a textbook, and a classroom that he had sat in as a student, not one he stood in front of as a teacher. All his ideas came from those more intelligent and more passionate than him. He then dismissed those individuals as quickly as he could so as not to arouse suspicion regarding their thoughts. He was the worst kind of human being. Better to be a murderer, a rapist, a pedophile than to be Ralph DiNardi. The murderers, rapists, and pedophiles at least have a sickness, an illness, a disease, perhaps. DiNardi was an opportunist who used the hard work and creativity of those who cared deeply against them while collecting a very lofty six-figure paycheck, utilizing an expense account, and driving around in a luxury sports car issued to him by the school.

Michael supposed he hated DiNardi so much because of his failure to support the hard work of those around him. He also hated him because DiNardi was a simpleton who thought he could cure everything wrong with the school and its community with a fucking hug and a fraudulent, well-placed pat on the shoulder. A year prior to this conversation, a female Spanish teacher, Janet Ecchevaria, was pushed down a flight of stairs by a young male student, Travis Hitchens, after she had reprimanded him for cutting her class in front of his girlfriend. Hitchens felt disrespected that he had been yelled at by a lady in front of his girl. Ecchevaria fell eleven steps. She fractured her clavicle, broke her nose, and received fourteen stitches to her forehead. She was in the hospital for a month, and it took her upward of seven months to gain enough mental and physical strength to return to work.

DiNardi gave the student a stern "talking to," and after meeting with his mother and having Travis wipe away his crocodile tears, he decided to keep the student in the school but placed him under probation. Coincidentally, one month later, the local paper printed a report about a young male student by the name of Travis Hitchens. It was reported that Hitchens was using the lavatory in his high school when he was beaten badly by a gang of students. Hitchens was put into a medically induced coma at the hospital. Police were asked by reporters how they knew it was gang activity. Captain Eliot Michaud's response: "No one person could have done this much damage to another individual on their own in such a limited amount of time. We assess there had to be at least three to four assailants."

A lengthy investigation ensued. No evidence was ever found. No arrests were ever made. No identification could be made. After Hitchens came out of his coma, the police asked him who it was who attacked him. He said he had no idea. He was attacked from behind, and he never saw anyone. He said it felt like five people were kicking him and punching him repeatedly. He said it felt like it was never going to end.

That night Father Sean Cloughey immediately called his brother. Father Cloughey did not know the most intimate goings-on of St. Catherine Preparatory High School. He didn't know anything about the curriculum, the teacher retention rates, or the student graduation ratio. What he did know was that St. Catherine Preparatory High School was a place completely devoid of any gang activity. He also knew that St. Catherine Preparatory employed his brother.

That was a little over two years ago.

So today when DiNardi looked at Michael and sighed, Michael broke his gaze and his eyes drifted to the wall over DiNardi's head. Centered above a credenza behind his enormous desk was DiNardi's diploma, which was framed in a cheap black plastic frame with a thin transparent sheet of plastic covering it. *Appropriate*, Michael thought. The largest desk he had ever seen was obviously overcompensating for DiNardi's lack of something—intelligence or penis length—and it made the already small diploma look like a shamefully framed postage stamp.

DiNardi, with his head propped up on his two fingers and palm, asked Michael to take him, step-by-step, through what exactly was running through his head during the events of his English literature class when he decided to punch Stanley Antoine, shattering his jaw in two places with one punch.

The nineteen-year-old Antoine was six-three, weighed 245 pounds, and he was a four-year letterman in football and hockey.

Michael said nothing. He looked down at his left hand, which was swollen and red, and the knuckles were severely bruised. The middle two knuckles were actually a mixture of deep purple and red from broken blood vessels. Previous cuts and gashes had left Michael with scars that, when red, also collected a yellow color about them in the corners. One of his shirtcuffs was tinged with a bit of something that possessed an orange-reddish hue that Michael mistook for a previous ketchup stain.

"Mr. Cloughey!" DiNardi said loudly. "Can you explain what happened in your classroom that would inspire a teacher of sixteen years to suddenly stand up, cross his room, and punch a student in the face? Are you listening to me?" DiNardi closed his eyes, took a deep breath, and put his hands together in front of his mouth in a steepled praying position. He desperately wanted Michael to say something, anything, even if it was incriminating.

He did not. He just looked at the watch on his right wrist.

CHAPTER 6

MICHAEL CLOUGHEY WAS NOT A BIG HUMAN BEING. He was never what one would define as intimidating. He realized at a very young age that the other kids around him were usually taller, heavier, and always seemed to be more masculine. He was always described as "skinny" or "tiny" or "scrawny." He came to hate the term "scrawny" the most. He could not remember a time when he did not feel self-conscious about his looks as well as his body image. In a house that was presided over by an Italian mother, scrawny was a curse. No matter how much he ate, how many workouts he participated in, or however many fat-inducing diets or protein shakes he attempted to digest, he never gained weight.

Throughout Michael's formative years and throughout high school, he played baseball. There was a period where he dreamed of baseball every night. It didn't seem to matter what his height or weight was while playing baseball. It was not basketball. It was not football. Baseball allowed him to think and show people how capable he was. He loved getting dirty and loved the idea of being part of a group of individuals that formed a bond, coming together to accomplish something. Maybe it was because he was a twin. Maybe it was just inherent. Maybe it was because he was never truly close to his father or his still living brother. Maybe it was because he was left-handed. When you are left-handed and you can pitch, the entire game revolves around you. This was something Michael cherished. He loved being revered on the baseball field. He loved the fact that someone on an opposing team would underestimate the scrawny pitcher with the skinny legs. It was fucking godlike. So, baseball became the thing he wanted to do all the time, and he did it well.

In Little League, he was always one step ahead of even the kids a year or two older than he was. He played for his church league when he wasn't playing for his Little League team. He became frustrated because kids his age proved to be no legitimate challenge. It was too easy. He was smarter and faster and had a better arm. He understood the game, and when a kid would make a mistake, he would walk up to that kid between innings and calmly tell the kid what to do the next time. He did this because he understood what it meant to be a good teammate, and he knew, more than most, that humans are prone to mistakes, especially while in the throes of pressure-inducing situations. He also did it because he hated losing. He imagined that losing was what death felt like.

By the time he reached high school, he had developed a reputation as one of the finest players in the city. He was called every hyperbole from a "fierce competitor" to a "spark plug" to a "dynamo." The reputation was justified. The labels, the accolades, the commentaries, and the newspaper articles were what he wanted and what he always craved. It quenched an incomprehensible thirst. His team would win and win often, and he was usually the main reason why. It would also become evident that the more attention he got on the baseball field, the more attention he got from the opposite sex. They looked past the skinny, scrawny frame. They saw something. They saw something...else. This made them want him more.

One afternoon when Lara shared with him what all the other girls were saying in her "How could not know that you idiot?" voice, he didn't know what to do with his thoughts. He never had a problem garnering the attention of girls, but this was like giving a bank robber a combination, a suitcase, and a two-hour head start in a sports car.

So, he played, and his team played behind him, and in his junior year of high school, they played for the state championship. Everyone showed up with the utmost of confidence that Michael would pitch them to the first championship in the history of their school. When Michael bent down in the first inning to pick up the baseball and face his catcher, he looked up and saw the faces of friends, girls he had become "friendly" with because of the very thing he was holding, his father, Yah, Sean, and Lara. For a moment, he felt guilty that he was the happiest to have Lara there above all the four thousand people watching the game.

He wasn't even nervous that several scouts representing professional teams were there to watch him and the opposing team's third baseman, David Mantinakis, go at it for a few hours. While his story was that he wasn't at all nervous the night before, Yah woke up to the sound of him throwing up his dinner, once at midnight and then again at 1:15 in the morning. When she asked if he was ok, he assured her he probably just had some sort of a stomach bug. The fact was that Michael was indeed incredibly nervous. He would never display it because to him that was weakness. These people came to see Michael Cloughey, not the skinny kid with the scrawny legs who couldn't hold down his mother's ravioli.

And so, the game went on, and both players lived up to expectations. In games such as this, one team usually establishes itself as the alpha and the other succumbs to their dominance. But this was not one of those games. This would be, to date, the most memorable high school game in the history of the state. By the time the seventh inning rolled around, both teams were fully aware of the event that was occurring around them. They were contributing to history. They were involved in something that transcended them as young human beings. Their names would be spoken of. The events of this day would be spoken to their children and the people of this state forever. It was not something they or their coaches were saying or using as fodder for motivation. They just felt it, and they were extremely correct for feeling it. It was baseball being played cleanly, with sophistication and polish. It was error-free and fun while also intense and, at times, nerve-racking.

This day would be remembered by everyone who was lucky enough to get a ticket. It would be remembered by those who shared the events of the game with friends or family. Unfortunately, it would not be remembered for what anyone did with a baseball, however. In the seventh inning with the score tied at 1–1, Michael walked the first batter of the inning on a questionable pitch on the outside corner. After mumbling a string of incoherent profanities about the umpire and his strike zone, he proceeded to strike out the next batter on three pitches.

Michael was irritated. Mantinakis was up, and he had already driven in the first run of the game with a triple. So far, he was winning the attention game. Mantinakis had spent the entire summer prior to this season getting ready for just such an occasion. There was not a moment that went by that he did not dream of getting a crack at Cloughey in the batter's box. He was tired of reading the articles and hearing his own coaches bestow praise on the opposing pitcher of tonight's game.

Michael, on the other hand, had a profound respect for his opponent tonight. Mantinakis was the reason the dinner would not stay down. Michael respected him and the player he was, and he also spent the entire spring reading articles about the young man who was about to walk up to the plate. In Mantinakis's first at-bat, Michael fell behind and he tried to coerce a fastball past him on the inside corner of the plate. When the pitch bled out over the middle, he delivered a triple into the right field corner, scoring the first player Michael had walked that game.

While at third base, he clapped and yelled to Michael, "I wipe my ass with your news articles, Cloughey."

This did not sit well with Michael, and he could feel a very familiar heat rising on the back of his neck. He felt his face reddening with anger. From row seven, seat sixteen, Sean saw it as well. Now Michael found himself in the same predicament as earlier. When Michael started to mumble about the missed strike call, Sean leaned over and whispered something in Lara's ear. Lara would never tell Michael what Sean said that day.

Mantinakis walked up to plate, expressionless. Michael knew he had to be incredibly careful here. He also knew he had to do something about the kid at first base before he threw a single pitch home. With Mantinakis in his stance, Michael threw over to first just to gauge distance. He threw over a second time to gauge the instincts of the runner. Mantinakis started laughing. He shook his head and settled in once again. Michael looked at the batter and shook off the catcher's first decision, which was a curveball. *It's easier to steal on a curve, Jimmy; everyone knows that.*

Out of the corner of his eye, he could see the runner on first pick up his heel and grind the front of his foot into the soft dirt off first base. Michael knew what this meant, and he knew that no one throws over to first base three times in a row. John Sr. sat up in his seat and wiped his forehead with the palm of his hand. His wife grabbed his other hand in hers. Michael looked at his catcher, momentarily said yes to a fastball, and shifted his weight to a full stop with his ball and glove resting at his waist. As he brought up his front leg, he saw the runner at first pick up his foot and slightly lean toward second base. Michael turned and delivered a throw to his first baseman so precise that the runner did nothing but stand still in place. After he was tagged out by the first baseman for the second out of the inning, he ran past Michael on his way to the dugout. As he did so, he said something to Michael. Whatever it was, Michael would never repeat to anyone, not even Lara. Sean didn't hear it, but he saw it and he understood that it was not conducive to this late day becoming a peaceful evening.

With two outs, Mantinakis, who had now waited a long time to see a pitch from Michael, looked at Michael with derision as he stood rooted in the batter's box. Now enraged, Michael threw the first pitch at Mantinakis's forehead. Mantinakis saw the ball that was about to end his life as his eyes opened to the size of half-dollars. He threw himself backward and ended up with the back of his uniform covered in dirt. When he got up,

Michael was staring at him with a look of contempt. Michael had received the ball back from his catcher, he had his glove under his arm, and he was rubbing up the ball. It was if he was saying, "I'll wait on you, Dave. Get cleaned up." What was once respect and competition to Michael was now torment and deep-seated hatred. Mantinakis got back in and took a deep breath.

Michael did not know it at the time, but he would throw only three more pitches as a baseball player. The first was a fastball on the inside corner of the plate that painted the black enough to be called a strike. Mantinakis, still startled by the prior experience, almost jumped out of his shoes at this pitch. The second was a curveball that started around Mantinakis's chest. By the time it crossed the plate, it was a little below knee height for strike two.

Michael felt good. He felt relieved that it was almost over. He actually felt big. He felt tall. He found a second to catch his breath and look at everything around him. The field, his friends, his family, and Lara all seemed to come into a sharpened view at the same time. It was a view without compromise. It lacked the fuzzy curiosity of a view encapsulated by tension, worry, or doubt. Michael took the ball, removed his glove again, and rubbed the ball diligently between both of his hands. He wanted to make sure that Mantinakis couldn't find even the slightest thing to use as an excuse for striking out. It was Michael's way of saying, "Here it is, Dave, you fuck. I even cleaned it for you!" Michael set himself and looked at his catcher, Jimmy Brennan. Brennan was one of Michael's best friends throughout high school, and years later he would attempt to tell this story to Michael's son at one reception and then again at his twelfth birthday party:

"So, I gave your dad the first sign for a curveball. Mantinakis was waitin' for a fastball. Your father shook me off, so I gave him the sign for a changeup. He shook me off again. I mean, I had no choice. So, I put down one and I moved to the outside corner of the plate. Your dad nodded his head yes, and he threw his pitch. All the air got sucked out of the park right then. I couldn't hear anything. Everything was going slow, like slow motion in the movies. I coulda swore the ball was in my glove. I mean, I felt it hit my glove, but then it was gone. Mantinakis let out this short grunt and he hit it. It just went."

Whenever he would tell that story, Jimmy would end up looking skyward by the end as if he could still see the flight of some imaginary baseball. It was at that point in the story that Lara would interrupt Jimmy and tell her son to go play with his friends.

On his way to first, Mantinakis blew Michael a kiss. On his way to second, he started clapping. On his way around third, he looked at Michael and winked. The place had erupted. John Sr. had his head in his hands. Yah had her eyes closed. Sean's hand was covering his mouth. Lara looked straight at Michael. Her eyes were solid and straight, but it appeared as if two diamonds had gained occupancy within the corners of both. Michael felt dizzy and slightly nauseous. He knew the game was over. Even though there were still two innings left, he knew it was all done. His arrogance had caused this. He should have listened to Jimmy and thrown the curveball.

The next batter would ground out on the second pitch hit weakly back to him for the third out. Between innings, Michael felt a collapse. He felt as though everything inside him was falling, sinking. But above all, he felt like killing someone. He walked into his dugout and placed his glove and cap down calmly under the section of the wooden bench that was parallel to first base. Michael had done this since he was seven when he dropped his glove in a park dugout and lost it. His father had spent an hour and a half lecturing him about the importance of awareness and taking care of his belongings. He stopped listening at one point, but he was very aware that the lecture ended with "Sean doesn't lose his shit."

Michael was due up second. He put on a batting helmet and picked up his bat. Thoughts about playing professional baseball were replaced by the feeling of him shrinking.

Sean would describe what followed that night with the accuracy of a machine: "*My brother put on his helmet and picked up his bat. I could see a fear inside him. I could feel a heat coming off him from where I was sitting. He took the bat in his left hand and ran across the field and into the opposing dugout. He dropped the bat and ran up to a young man. It was the kid Dave. My brother punched him in the face twice. He punched him very hard and very fast. When he fell down, Michael picked up his bat and swung as hard as he could across Dave's leg. He did it twice. It took four people to pull him off the kid. He was screaming and his eyes were red, and his mouth was full of spit. His lips and teeth and tongue were bundled into a snarl like a dog with its defenses up. It was one of the most difficult things I have ever witnessed.*"

John Sr. and his wife stood holding each other while their son turned into the proverbial werewolf right in front of them. Virginia started crying and covering her face with her hands. Sean was screaming Michael's name mingled with "Stop!" "Mike!" "Don't!" and "No!" The diamonds that had settled in Lara's eyes were now migrating south down her face. She had obviously seen Michael angry before but not quite under these circumstances or to this unimaginable extent. It was like being forced to continuously watch a car accident.

And that was it. It was all over with. According to the watch resting on the wrist of John Sr., the whole skirmish lasted for a little over ten minutes from the time Michael got the last batter to ground out to when Michael was carried back into his dugout kicking and screaming. That was it. Just ten minutes for the state, Michael's family, Lara, and for two professional baseball scouts to see what a skinny, scrawny kid with chicken legs from Brooklyn was capable of. The scout for the Chicago Cubs shook his head, closed his notebook, and placed it in his small leather attaché. He held a pained expression on his face throughout all of it before getting up and shifting his way out of his row to exit the small stadium.

When you think of the determined and passionate rage to hurt someone and the actual physical commitment it takes to carry those actions out, you never develop the mental picture of a kid that looks like Michael Cloughey. You reserve a space on the wall in your mind where you hang a portrait of a hulking, gruesome, and ominous mass of humanity. You do not picture a five-foot, eight-inch kid who weighs 137 pounds when his pockets are filled with rocks.

So, seeing this made all the accolades, the praise, and the prestige depart faster than a mild day in February.

While Michael's temper was never a deep, dark secret to those very close to him, particularly Sean, that night it was a neon billboard for everyone to look at and address in their own way. Suffering the effects of this incident lay David Mantinakis on his back. Dave suffered a broken kneecap and a vivid collection of bruises, welts, and deep cuts, the scars of which would last him his entire life, especially the mental ones.

This would be the last baseball game that both Michael and David would ever play. David Mantinakis would never be able to walk again without the assistance of a cane nor sufficiently throw with his right hand.

When Michael was seven years old, he lost his glove in a park baseball field dugout. And during a state championship, Michael Cloughey lost his shit in front of everyone who cared to watch, and this cost him an opportunity that only offers itself to a select few young men with skills that Yah would ironically describe to John Sr. as God-given.

That would be Michael's last baseball game.

CHAPTER 7

As PLAYGROUNDS ARE CONCERNED, KIDS FALL INTO several categories. Some kids are into slides, some are into monkey bars, the more questionable and perhaps expeditious youngsters love the sandbox. The elite playground attendees favor the swings. The swings speak to the adventurous souls who throw safety and acrophobia out the window. The swings are for the true playground warriors—the highlanders. The swings are for the risk-takers and the courageous. Alexander the Great, Napoleon Bonaparte, Thomas Jefferson, Julius Caesar, and Douglas MacArthur would have been frequent visitors to the swing section of the playground. Albert Einstein would have been a monkey bar kid. Fredrich Nietzsche would have gravitated to the slides. Erwin Rommel—definitely a sandbox kid. Most politicians would have focused heavily on the abusive and ironic seesaw section, which, by its mere presence, defines uncertainty, slight reluctance, and trepidation. They would be the kid who got the opposing seesaw participant to the top and then jumped off to leave the other crashing to the ground, feeling that most disconcerting stinger that starts at your tailbone and ends up finishing off someplace in your lower brain stem—sons of bitches.

Michael Cloughey didn't like the swings; he adored them with a passion most kids reserve for ice cream and their favorite sweets. Michael loved to swing and considered himself a proud champion of the activity. At the ripe age of seven, he was proficient in the fully seated and squatting positions. He even perfected the standing position and showed it off with a grace and precision unmatched by most kids twice his age. However, above all things, Michael loved what became known in most playgrounds as "twosies." Twosies was when one kid would sit on the swing, and another would stand over them on the same swing. Their collective power would make them gather such speed and height that they could practically spin the swing over its metal joint at the crossbar top. Twosies required two things:

Complete disregard for personal safety, health, and human well-being.

A partner either idiotic enough or brave enough to undertake this deadly task with you.

Michael had run the gamut of inequitable partnerships regarding twosies. Some partners were too timid for his taste, some lacked the coordination, and some were overambitious in their ascent. One partner, Howard Euchin, Michael's grammar school gym buddy, was the least successful in his attempt to qualify for a suitable twosies partner. At about two minutes into the swing, he threw up all over himself. Michael was highly grateful he insisted that Howard be seated for this tryout.

One extremely humid July day just a touch past the huge Fourth celebration, Yah took Michael to the playground for the sprinklers and for some ice cream. Both Michael and Yah agreed that the only way to go regarding ice cream flavors was pistachio. The fact that it was green only made it better to Michael. While hogging up the much sought-after shady bench in the playground, Michael could see the swings. He could see a few older kids gathering and talking, and he surmised they were impressed by something. They seemed to be laughing and jumping around and throwing their hands up in the air. These wild gesticulations could only mean one thing: a rival. Michael leaned over to Yah, who had fallen asleep under the relief that the mist from the sprinkler mixed with the shade the cypress tree had provided.

He whispered, "Be right back."

He was so enrapt in the activity of the older kids and what was before them he hadn't even noticed his ice cream had melted and fallen out of the cone. He was walking with an empty sugar cone in his hand with its impatient remnants running down his closed fingers and the inside of his dirty palm. He also hadn't been sure, but he was now certain that one of the older kids gathering and observing this spectacle was Sean. Sean had spent a lengthy portion of this summer growing and eating most of whatever John and Virginia filled the refrigerator and pantry with. He was usually always able to identify Sean in any large crowd, but with his unchallenged charge toward a height of beyond six feet and his unrelenting, swirling cowlick, he was now a dead giveaway for any police lineup constructed.

"Mikey?"

"What's this?"

"You here with Mom?"

"Yeah, what is this? Who is that?"

"I dunno. Pretty good, right?"

"Yeah."

"Why you got an empty ice cream cone?"

"You want some?"

"Mikey, it's empty. Why you holding it?"

Michael looked down at the cone and back up at Sean. "I dunno."

"You know what, Mikey? I think you got some competition, kid."

Some familiar voice in the background echoed Sean's statement. It supported Sean's opinion emphatically while chuckling almost simultaneously. Michael understood the chuckle as an insult and tried to frame the speaker with his eyes. He could not. What he could see clearly, too clearly, was that his brother was right. This young Amelia Earhart was just as good, if not better, than he was. This was a fact he would never admit publicly. She appeared fearless. She was an astronaut, a term he only applied to the highest and most revered members of the playground swing crew. She had balance, determination, and sophistication on the swing. James Joyce would have defined her as "the embodiment of grace." She was also a total stranger, an enigma. Where did this girl come from? Why had he never seen her before? Why had she entered his sacred arena and thrown down this unmitigated challenge of "Swing Master of the Universe"?

He was immediately bothered to his very core by this. What started out as a most pleasant summer day with Yah at the park turned into an upheaval of emotion. Uncertainty and doubt filled his head, and he felt the need, the desire to hit something and scream until his ears bled. Michael was most upset by the fact that this newcomer had literally swung her way into his life. He was also upset by the fact that his own brother, his very own older brother, had said something out loud in front of the masses when he could have offered it up to Michael while alone or at dinner. Dinner tonight was going to consist of pork chops with apples and homemade mashed potatoes. That seemed like a highly appropriate meal to deliver this earth-shattering report of current affairs.

Michael immediately asked himself what he should do. He mentally sought out the guidance of his childhood hero, the Lone Ranger. What would the Lone Ranger do? When faced with a true and obvious challenge, how would he and his partner, Tonto, handle torment such as this? Would he be diplomatic and sidle up to his foe and use his charm to save face? Or would he come out, six-guns blazing, and ask the questions after the carnage was complete? All Michael knew was that he had to do something and do it quickly.

He had two choices. The first was to call out this heathen and challenge her to a competition. Michael didn't really know what the word "heathen" meant, but he heard it spoken at church a few times and it seemed somewhat dark enough to be used at this given moment in this context. The second option would be to befriend this fellow lover of swings and make her his twosies partner. He decided to feel out the situation and make the proper introductions before a rather rash decision was made. As he walked over to his young competitor, he wiped the visible sweat from his forehead and upper lip, and he realized that he had close to an entire mustache consisting of crusty pistachio ice cream. He quickly turned to tend to his appearance when he heard a raspy voice from behind.

"Hey, you!" it clawed out.

Somewhere in Michael's head, he felt a *thud!*

"Hey!" the voice called again.

He knew this bellow was aimed at him, and to have turned and faced its caller with a visible ice cream mustache would have placed him at an even larger disadvantage. This never would have happened to the Lone Ranger. Michael turned and saw his foe. Except she was about twenty feet above him. She was swinging so high that he swore she would come down with icicles attached to her. The entire crowd was hushed as she entered a different atmosphere. She did this while retaining a fixed gaze on Michael Cloughey. For the first time in his young life, Michael knew he had been bested. Sean whispered something in his ear, but Michael didn't hear it. All he knew was that it ended with "Jesus Christ." Michael locked eyes with this girl.

Lara Louise Trammell was raven-haired, and her eyes were a dark green. They were a balanced mixture of emerald and light gray. She was skinny, and her complexion was a delicate sun-kissed pink from her time spent outdoors that summer. This would fade during the winter, and Lara would present slightly less than ivory. Her long black hair accented this presentation. She had dirty knees and elbows, and her torn denim shorts and beat-up Chuck Taylor sneakers suggested she only had the one pair and they were doing their yeoman's share of work. In all, Lara Trammell displayed an intimidating appearance for most boys, even the older ones. Michael Cloughey knew at that moment they would be friends for a very long time.

She slowed down her swing and jumped off in midair at the end of her performance like a damn superhero. She was rugged and sweet, and for years Michael adored the idea that she could wear a smudge of dirt as adorably and confidently as some women wear blush. She walked right over to Michael and said, "I'm Lara." Michael was flabbergasted at this confident and rather tomboyish girl.

"I'm Michael."

"I know. You're good." The fact that she knew this and could already identify him made his stomach feel odd.

"Yeah, I love the swings."

"The other kids here talk about you. They say you're the best."

"I've never seen you here."

"Just moved here. Been here for about two weeks."

"Oh."

"Are you here a lot?"

"Yeah, most days with my brother or Ya—Mother."

"Well, I have to go. My dad is waiting."

"Okay. Bye."

And before she ran off, she licked the tip of her left thumb and extended it toward the bottom of Michael's right cheek, removing the remaining evidence of pistachio ice cream. The odd feeling in Michael's stomach grew.

CHAPTER 8

THE NEXT DAY AND FOR A SUCCESSION OF THIRTEEN more, Michael found himself at the park on the swings with Lara Trammell. It would make little to no difference who would chaperone his visits. Yah and Sean both took turns, and both ran out of gas quickly enough. On the occasion that Yah had things to do, Michael would beg until she was just worn out from hearing his pleas and promises. When Sean had things to do, he would harass Sean until he would give in.

One day Sean had simply had enough, and he bent down slightly, looked at Michael in the eye, and screamed in his face, "*No!*"

Michael abruptly turned, walked down the hallway, and slammed the door as he entered his room. He took one of his long worn-out white knee-high socks. He then took three other socks and a blue Spalding handball and shoved them all into each other. When the apparatus developed the look of some medieval torture device, Michael carried it, dragging it along the floor, in the direction of Sean's room. Michael peacefully knocked on the door, and when Sean opened it, Michael wedged his left foot in the doorway and pushed the door open with his left shoulder. As Sean stepped backward, Michael slipped through the door using a quickness that only a deep and longing desire could summon. He swung the makeshift flail with all his might, striking Sean in the shoulder once. As Sean fell backward, he readied his aim again and caught Sean in the stomach. The sound was a thick and muddy thump that had a rubbery, springy *boing* to it at the end. It was followed by the sounds of Sean's gasping for air and coughing uncontrollably.

"Stop! Okay! Stop, Mike!"

Neither Yah nor John Sr. could ever deduce what drove their son to such primal fits of unexplainable rage. There were several theories, but no one was ever able to exactly put their finger on it. No one was ever able to curb it either, except for Lara. John Sr. blamed his son's ferocity on his wife's family. He claimed that Michael took after Virginia's oldest brother, Luca. Luca was a butcher in Sicily, and he never made the trip with the family to America. He was imprisoned for the murder of his wife and her lover. The Italian police, the carabiniere, found the body of Silvizio DeTucco in the freezer of Luca's butcher shop hanging next to two decapitated pigs and three sides of beef. They found Luca's wife at home in bed with her arms tied to the corner of each bedpost and her feet and knees tied together. This would not have been so bad had she not been made to lay there in that position for two months. The Italian newspapers printed the headline, "*Il Macellaio l'hafatto!*"—"The Butcher Did It!"

It was a story the LaPietra family wished to avoid like an unpinned grenade, and it was the major reason for their sudden departure to America. The tragic incident scarred the entire LaPietra family and acted as a wedge between family members. How does a clan ever truly recover from a familial earthquake such as that? The fallout was deep and painful. The Italian press knew no bounds when trying to unearth the history and background of Luca LaPietra. Virginia was always fearful that one of her children would be born with the volatile and restless spirit of Luca. Luca was always hot-blooded, and when it came to matters of the heart, he was prepared to fight to the death. "*Dio, patria, e famiglia!*" (God, country, and family) were the overly dramatic words he screamed as he was being carried out of an Italian courtroom by four officers. To many who contemplated the death scene, Luca's wife was posed to resemble Christ on the cross. It was believed he tied her up so she could live in eternity repenting for her infidelity and being punished for her sins. Criminals were crucified and displayed so as to be a symbol to those who gazed upon them that their actions would not be tolerated or condoned. Those who read the newspaper assumed that Luca wanted his wife to be a sign for all other women even contemplating an affair.

In actuality, Luca arrived home to find his wife and her lover in medias res. Her hands were tied to the bedposts with two silk bathrobe straps, and her legs were spread to be able to tie each ankle to the footboard posts. When Luca arrived home early and entered their bedroom, his eyes immediately landed on the back of her lover's head and shoulders as they were parked but idling heavily between his wife's legs. Luca felt every bit of fury he ever possessed rise in him as he pounced, first killing his wife's lover so she could observe what she had caused. Later, when he was done with his wife, he left her hands tied to the posts of the headboard, but he would close her legs and secure them tightly from upper thigh through to the ankle. This was not to replicate a crucifixion, but so that there would not be a man in the afterlife ever capable of entering his wife. It would be that scene and that type of unbridled fury that the LaPietra family would be identified with. In their town, their region, their country, and their language, the name LaPietra translated to "the stone." In one afternoon, Luca LaPietra changed that translation and its association with any type of earthly element. This is what Luca's cry of "God, country, and family" was meant to convey to everyone who could hear it being bellowed from the deepest part of his chest.

Virginia knew Sean was much too kind-hearted and gentle in spirit to have any traces of Luca LaPietra embedded in his soul. Michael was different, however. Michael was prone to fits of wild temper and extreme bouts of rage. Even as an infant, Michael would become overly frustrated and enraged about the discomforts of a wet diaper, hunger, or lack of sleep. Sean, for instance, would sob so much when he was hungry that he often fell asleep right in the middle of a meal out of exhaustion. Michael was markedly different than any child John Sr. had ever come in contact with. Michael would turn red and expel this sound that was low and guttural. He would curl his small hands into fists and seemingly punch at imaginary figures in front of him. Michael's teething episodes were equivalent to exorcisms. John Sr. knew that all children ran through their course of nature during their infancy and formative years. However, Michael Cloughey was a tornado, a hurricane, and a tsunami delivered in an extremely tiny package.

With all these detectable oddities, there was still something about Michael that was charming, appealing, and even sweet in disposition. Virginia witnessed Michael as a child performing acts of kindness. She watched him helping around the house as best as he could. He didn't even have to be asked to clean up his room. One day, Virginia was looking out the front window without Michael realizing she was there. She saw Michael in front of their house tossing a baseball several stories high only to pretend he was making the last out of a baseball game. Their elderly next-door neighbor, Betty Amodio, nicknamed Aunt B by John Sr., was carrying in groceries from her cart, and Michael stopped, put down his ball and glove, and helped Aunt B carry in the five heavy, bulging bags. When she offered to give Michael some change as a tip, the boy refused and said he just wanted to help her. So, Virginia struggled with this idea of how a boy who possessed Michael's likability could be prone to such a different side to his demeanor.

Even with the highly plausible explanation of a Luca LaPietra and a very volatile component buried within Michael's chemical composition, Virginia chose to apply a less "moviesque" and macho course of reasoning for Michael's bouts of rage and bloody vengeance, perhaps out of naivete or perhaps out of a refusal to see the truth. She would explain that the Cloughey household was a home of extremes when it came to parenting strategy. John Sr. was quiet and determined and taught his boys to be men through self-discipline and control while she taught them how to embrace life with passion and a tireless creativity. Virginia's love for art, music, and literature was only compounded by her love of food and red wine.

John Sr. would see a dilemma and work his way out of it. John Sr. would carefully plot his way from Point A through Point Z, accounting for variables and creating contingencies. Virginia would see the same problem and try to poetically step her way out of it. She believed that love and devotion were solutions in and of themselves. It was not the greeting card type of love that she attempted to evoke. It held a deeper meaning, and it connected more to existence, being, soul. Virginia honestly felt that Michael was torn. He wanted to resolve his issues and solve his problems. He wanted closure; however, he was cursed with the "confusion of passion," as she called it. Michael's blood would practically ignite when he met with resistance and conflict. It was this confusion that led to Michael being unable to cope with life at times.

John Sr. called that a "bullshit excuse." He loved his boys but saw something very black, very dangerous, within Michael. All he knew was that there weren't any murderers lurking in the Irish side of Michael's family tree. The Clougheys of County Kilkenny, Ireland, were farmers, as were their ancestors before them. John Sr. knew of no alarming traits present in his background. His childhood trips to Ireland were most memorable due to fresh milk, eggs, and buttered tea biscuits. You worked hard and were fed until the sun went down, and then when it came up, you collected eggs, milked cows, and began the process all over again. You appreciated it all because you worked or helped to make the ingredients on your plate a possibility. If you were good, you found bacon on your plate from a pig that met its demise the day before. It was good living, clean living. Life was simple. Actions were humble, as were most of the people you encountered.

John Sr. grew to understand the significance of basic need and necessity. He knew the difference between giving your children what they desired versus giving them what they needed to exist. In his world, excess was dangerous and only led to consistently being unhappy with what you had. He promised himself he would never spoil his children to the point that they would not appreciate the smallest offerings of kindness. To have children with no expectation of reward or gain was proper parenting. Small acts or gestures of nicety were fine, such as a candy bar or an extra soda here or there, but John Sr. preferred his children modest and unassuming. At the end of the day, the goal was to leave your kids with enough money to do something in life but not so much money as to be able to do nothing.

In Sean, John Sr. saw an unassuming boy who accepted his younger brother's punishments with understanding. Sean easily could have curbed Michael's torture of him. Sean could have grabbed Michael and throttled him until he broke. Sean easily could have bested Michael physically. He simply chose not to. Sean never touched Michael in an aggressive manner. He never once lashed out through fatigue, frustration, or impatience. He seemed to just accept his brother and realize that it was his very inherent nature that made him act this way. This worried John Sr. immensely. Perhaps if Sean had smacked Michael around when he was younger, there would be no such comparisons to Luca LaPietra. If Sean had just given Michael one good shot to the head at an early age, then maybe John Sr. wouldn't worry so much about his youngest boy. But that never happened. Sean never did, and neither did John Sr.

John Sr. was a big man. He possessed a freakish physical strength that matched his mental fortitude. For a man who worked behind a desk most of his days and never performed any real hard labor save for common household repairs, he was a healthy specimen of muscle mixed with height. He attributed this to his ancestors and their tilling, plowing, and eating of healthy and hearty foods. John Sr. was disciplined as a child, as were his six siblings. If you were disobedient, you met with a leather belt or the full, fleshy calloused hand of your father. Cursing was met with a mouth filled with a bar of soap. It was what was done. It was generally acceptable parenting. John Sr. never looked back at his childhood as abusive. He did know one thing, however. Michael was too small and too thin to be hit by John Sr. He was honestly afraid to touch his son for fear he might damage him. It was certainly not out of the realm of possibility. He never had to hit Sean. Sean never did anything to warrant punishment. This also worried John Sr. somewhat— one son who was so admirably obedient with the Holy Spirit standing next to him and another who had a hurricane trapped inside of him. How could he have had two children who were so completely different in nature and spirit and demeanor? So, John Sr. worried about his youngest boy. He figured every parent lost sleep due to the wild happenings of their children, but Michael Cloughey took years off his father's life. If he couldn't blame the blood of Luca LaPietra, then who could he blame? Maybe the stone had landed on Michael, causing his life to be just a little bit too heavy.

CHAPTER 9

DiNardi sighed again. He extended his right arm to pick up a large gray mug with the strings of two tea bags rolling over the side and wrapped around the handle. The tags identified the delicate beverage as decaffeinated English breakfast tea. DiNardi lightly blew into the cup and took a conservative sip from it. He began as he lowered the mug from his face. "I just don't know what would possess you to do such a ridiculous thing. You're a good teacher, Michael. Your departmental supervisor constantly argues that you're the best English teacher he has ever worked with. He has even admitted that you should probably be the departmental chair, not him."

Michael raised his eyes up to meet DiNardi's. He felt tired. Not sleepy tired. Not the kind of tired you feel when you have been on a long excursion. Not even the kind of tired you feel when you have toiled at a labor of love. Michael felt exhausted in a different way, an unexplainable way. His head felt heavy, his shoulders felt poorly postured, and his eyes felt like clos-ing—not sleeping, just closing. He would have given anything to be horizontal. He mostly felt confused. Not confused by what he had done. Michael Cloughey was confused by what he was and what he had always been.

"To walk up to a student and spontaneously punch him in the face seems like an insane action. Are you insane, Michael? Please tell me you have had a break with some aspect of reality, and I will tell the boy's parents and the police, who are on their way here to meet with you and your union representative."

Michael thought of Lara. How would he explain this? What would he tell his wife? How do you phrase all of this in a "just got home" conversation?

"Hey, how was your day?"

"Fine"

"How about yours?"

"Good, I picked up the dry cleaning, got some stuff at the gro-cery store, and I punched one of my students in the face. He will be having all his meals for the next two months through a straw. Oh, and by the way, I will probably be arrested and imprisoned for a brief period. Oh, and even better, we will be incurring a shitload of legal debt from my adventures this morning."

"Are you on drugs, Michael? Are you on antidepressants? Are you an alcoholic? Did you drink today? Are you suffering from some illness we should all be made very much aware of? How about illegal stuff? Anything? I have to be able to justify this somehow, and you're not helping me with this no speak bullshit!" DiNardi's anger was growing, and his patience was clinging precipitously to any word Michael wished to even-tually offer up to the gods. DiNardi wasn't upset with what Michael had done. He wasn't upset that Michael was sitting in front of him. He wasn't even upset that Michael hadn't even made eye contact with him. He was upset at how this would reflect upon him. How this would challenge his ability to lead and how people viewed him as a leader.

Ralph DiNardi was a window dresser. He seemed mostly concerned with the look, appearance, and perception of his school. If the back of the school were on fire, he would only be concerned if you could see the black plume of smoke from the front. Substance, content, and validity were not words that entered his pedagogy. Each kid was a dollar sign, and each kid represented a continuation of a long-ago status the school once held. It lived off its antiquated reputation of academic excellence, and DiNardi was the gatekeeper of that reputation. The mahogany, ceramic tile, and polyester blazers were like the curtain on a very expensive Broadway musical. The audience recognized the theater and the stage as brilliant, glittering, and sensational to the senses, the eyes and ears in particular. However, from backstage you got the opportunity to see the cracks, the tape holding things together, the fragility of its existence. DiNardi answered primarily to the board of trustees and the incredibly wealthy donors that bled money into its endowment. In DiNardi's opinion, anyone that did not recognize a school, any school, as a business was useless. The school itself was twenty kinds of fucked up. Fiscal mismanagement, lack of efficiency, and lack of educational vision ruled the day. If the young men and women who walked the halls did not already enter the school extremely gifted and beyond motivated, the building would have shuttered and been sold to an enormous real estate company for a high number followed by seven zeros.

However, good old Ralph and his experienced twenty-five plus years in marketing and advertising kept everything at bay and the money flowing. He kept all the negative imagery and subpar performances internalized. No one was able to see the real school. The rare visitor was treated to three-course lunches and met with floor plans and blueprints for projects that never really existed. Most of the wealthy donors only really wanted three things (in order of how truly empty, base, and fucked-up the donor was):

To satisfy their accountants and financial planners with sizable donations to not-for-profit organizations.

To support the historically prestigious and extremely successful football team.

To feel some minor sense of decency after spending a humongous portion of their time and wealth totally fucking people out of their time and wealth.

After the final checks were all written and signed, the need to stop by was not high on the list of fraudulent priorities of the bloated donors themselves. The "So-and-so" Library. The "So-and-so" Science Lab. The "So-and-so" Arts Center.

The projects that Headmaster DiNardi, his actual title, did financially back and put into play were ineffective, and a core group of teachers suspected DiNardi was getting an obscene kickback from construction, electrical, and plumbing companies all over the state. DiNardi drove two different high-end luxury cars on a rotating basis. He had a beautiful home and once bragged about a summer house someplace warm. Someone rumored it was in Costa Rica. When Lara and Michael attended a faculty / board member fundraiser one winter, Lara whispered in Michael's ear that DiNardi's suit cost an estimated two thousand dollars. Lara could stop a parade and inform Michael, almost to the dollar, what the high-stepping band leader was wearing and its price. Her eye never failed when it came to fashion, and in DiNardi's case, she was probably spot-on in her estimation. The frustrating thing to Michael was that DiNardi wore a suit like that one almost every single day, and it didn't seem as though he repeated one.

So, on this day DiNardi wasn't truly upset with Michael for punching a student twice his size in the face during his English class. DiNardi, as most adults at St. Catherine, disliked Stanley Antoine immensely. What he was extremely angry with was that his magic trick of a school was going to be revealed for what it was. In DiNardi's view, there was nothing worse than finding out how the magician made the six-thousand-pound elephant disappear from the huge glass case. Well, an even bigger trick here would be keeping all the interested parties at arm's length when this shitty current event hit the police desk, the newspapers, and the family of a one Stanley Antoine.

Antoine's parents were Cuban and Haitian. They were very dedicated immigrants and came here primarily to provide a life for their son and daughter they could never have in their native Haiti. America provided them with the opportunity to live a productive life and give their children an education that was safe, free, and lacking any sort of political affiliation unless you dedicated yourself to one. Mr. Antoine was a mortgage officer at a highly regarded bank. He had started as a teller. Mrs. Antoine was a vice president of guest relations at a very upscale hotel in the heart of Times Square. She had started there as a cleaning woman while taking evening classes at Pace University. She had finished the fifth grade in her native Cuba before her family took advantage of the rare and dangerous opportunity to escape Castro and his political reign. They settled in Jacksonville and over the course of years moved their way up the East Coast. At the age of twenty-two, Racquel Castillo, her two sisters, and their parents eventually found themselves moving in with their cousin in East Flatbush, Brooklyn. Five years later, after meeting Stanley Antoine Sr. through a friend, they would be married, and she would become Mrs. Stanley Antoine.

Between their respective homelands and their modest and admirable ascent in the United States, they were not strangers to struggle, to pain, to uprising. They were certainly not strangers to the concepts of patience and hard work. They were also not strangers to corporal punishment as it had been doled out to both of them as children, especially at school. The questioning of a teacher was just not done, ever. Bad things happened to those who questioned authority. It was better to accept whatever punishment was attached to a wrong then to bring attention to yourself. Attention, negative attention, in Haiti and Cuba usually meant disappearance, pain, and injustice.

However, how could the Antoine's, having fought their entire lives to free themselves from the bindings of unfairness, feel that good old spirit of approval knowing their son had been punched in the face by his English teacher? One of the things the Antoine's appreciated about their son's school was that it was safe from the gangs that plagued the daily existence of their immediate environs. How do you sincerely explain to parents that their son was attacked, not by a gang of thugs initiating a new member, but by his teacher? His rather diminutive English teacher?

Stanley had been recruited by St. Catherine's to major in two sports and help carry on the long tradition of success. If it were not for football, the Antoine's, even with their upper middle-class salaries, could never afford the thirty-five-thousand-dollar yearly tuition. His math and English grades were not actually a priority, nor a consideration. They were a rather thin spoke in a very rugged wheel.

DiNardi rubbed his forehead. He had deep creases and lines that ran from east to west across it. He sipped his tea once more and then looked at Michael as if Michael were a coma patient you visited in the hospital. You are told to engage coma patients in conversation just in case they can hear or sense your presence, but you're pretty sure there is absolutely nothing going on behind the fleshy underbelly of those closed eyelids.

"Do you have anything to say?"

"Do you want to make any sort of statement?"

"Do you want to write anything down, Michael?"

"Do you want your delegate?"

"Jesus Christ."

DiNardi picked up the receiver on his desk phone and began making the phone call he never wanted to make, never thought he would have to make, never suspected he would have to make.

DiNardi was about to attempt to make the elephant disappear.

CHAPTER 10

ROBERT HANOVER PICKED UP THE PHONE IN HIS office after his special assistant informed him it was "pressing." He had developed this phrase and its understanding with her over the course of years working together. The special assistant was, in his opinion, the most difficult of all positions in his corporation to fill and hold on to. It required an unmatched trust and a loyalty equivalent to an attorney on retainer, a medical specialist, and a longtime therapist combined into one human being. A special assistant was not a secretary or a gopher. Those terms insulted the craft, and it acted as an insinuation that all Anya Crawford did for him was simply fetching coffee or hiding his sexual liaisons. Anya always did the second, but Hanover, as she called him, refused to ever ask her to do the first. It would be a pure insult to her more specialized skills.

Hanover was fully aware of the fact that the wrong special assistant or a random assistant who could not be trusted could destroy a man of his wealth, power, and varied proclivities. So he and Anya developed a professional relationship that never entered any other realm. They became professionally friendly with an understanding of boundaries. Over the course of their thirteen-year relationship, they also developed a vernacular all their own. It was a shorthand that they both understood and never questioned. Ms. Crawford, as he called her, was compensated extremely well in every way. Economically, she was rewarded for the taking on of extra assignments, which meant she would lie to his wife for him and admit he was at a meeting he could simply not be pulled away from. This meant he was enjoying the company of a woman or women he was spoiling in large and a varied number of ways. Ms. Crawford was also treated to a company car of her choosing. This was always renewed every two years with an upgraded model. Ms. Crawford's car of choice was always the BMW. Although Hanover tried to lure her into choosing a Mercedes, a Maserati, or even a Jaguar, Anya always preferred the BMW. She felt it was a perfect match for her, just enough car for her diminutive stature and sophisticated tastes. One day Anya arrived at her desk and found it covered in brochures for some of the most expensive cars on the planet, none of which were a BMW. This was Hanover's "subtle" way of telling her it was time to choose another vehicle. She gathered the brochures and wrapped them in a giant red and gold ribbon and inserted a small, typed note that read:

Hanover,

As with some people in this office, I do not feel the need to overcompensate for my numerous shortcomings.

Ms. Crawford

She placed the pile on Robert's desk for his arrival. When he saw the pile and read the note, he immediately smiled and broke out into laughter that lasted for at least five minutes. He gave her the entire day off as an apology for the insult. She refused to take the day off. He knew that her joke was a small but serious hint that the lady always knew what she wanted, and he should have known better than to try to make her compromise it.

The car, the all-expenses-paid vacations, the wardrobe allowance, and expense accounts were all just part of the perks of working for a man like Robert Hanover. He was one of the wealthiest and most sought-after men in the world. His business scope and acumen were recognized both on national and international scales. Robert Hanover obtained his legal degree from Georgetown University and his degree in corporate finance from Cornell University. It was this level of intelligence and determination that put him in good stead with federal agencies such as the CIA and DEA. His own business was sought after for healing and resuscitating large-scale corporations that were on the verge of bankruptcy and collapse. Robert Hanover was called a corporate healer, and the United States government asked his company to get corporations that were deemed necessary to the well-being of the nation back on their feet. If this meant he would have to contribute the actual money himself, create a financial plan, and get his payback later, then so be it. He dined with some of the most influential human beings on the planet. He frequently met with politicians, Washington insiders, corporate power players, and the occasional Hollywood mogul. The need, desire, and insistence for privacy, secrecy, and peace of mind were of utmost importance. Ms. Crawford provided all of this and more. She was able to interpret and distinguish between a friendly call from a Midwestern senator just touching base and the desperate, hushed tone of a foreign dignitary who was about to be arrested and in need of a quick fix to make a sexual scandal or coup disappear. Those calls made it through immediately and in their shared vernacular were called "nukes."

The need for unmitigated trust was at the very top of the food chain in Robert Hanover's world, and Anya provided a quiet disconnect that never judged his needs or wants. As a matter of fact, aside from his desire and passion for women, the busy mogul only spent time focusing on two things. Robert Hanover was a celebrated collector of all things Civil War. He was an avid Civil War buff and extensively researched the period himself. He was not a three-day weekend reenactment guy, no costumes needed or wanted. Mr. Hanover truly had an affection for that particular conflict and its effects on the United States as it stood now. He would often work small statistics and Civil War facts into conversations with very unsuspecting people who did not deem him to be a history fan. On one trip to Paris, he spent four hours talking to Ms. Crawford about Lincoln's presidential cabinet and how and why it was filled with some of his biggest adversaries. Doris Kearns Goodwin he was not, but he lulled Anya to sleep with stories of Antietam and Gettysburg.

The third and possibly most coveted passion in the world of Robert Hanover was his old high school, St. Catherine Preparatory High School. It was at St. Catherine that Robert Hanover connected with a history teacher, Mr. Felix Abramson. It was during Robert's sophomore year when Abramson inspired him through his daily lessons and focus on 1860–1865 and all that went into it. Robert was hooked, and it led to a lifelong passion for history and how we need it more than it needs us. Robert considered teaching and following in the footsteps of Mr. Abramson. If it were not for an extremely large trust fund with a clause demanding he study finance or law, Robert would have been a passionate history teacher.

When Mr. Abramson retired, Robert anonymously paid for him and his family to go on an all-expenses-paid vacation to Europe. He also had his people add fifty thousand dollars to Mr. Abramson's rather modest pension fund. When Mr. Abramson died of complications due to diabetes, Robert stepped up and led a campaign of donors to rename the library at St. Catherine's "The Felix S. Abramson Historic Library." It was rebuilt and filled with some of the finest research tools any university would be proud to have. All except for the original copy of the Declaration of Independence could be found hanging on one of its walls. This was a project that even Ralph DiNardi couldn't skirt around. St. Catherine's had built itself the nicest high school library in the nation, all thanks to Robert Hanover and his "elves," another shorthand term used by Hanover and Ms. Crawford.

Over the years Robert and his small contingent of very generous donors had contributed over eighteen million dollars to St. Catherine's. Much of that went to scholarships, endowments, and facility enhancements. The only difference between Robert and some of the other donors was that Mr. Hanover expected results when he contributed funds. He showed up to ask questions, and he had everyone from his own private engineer team to his financial officers provide critical input. Anything that made the school better or more admirable worked for Robert Hanover's portfolio.

If he had not been so busy in his own life, he would have sat on the board of trustees at St. Catherine and fired Ralph DiNardi himself. He could not bring himself to trust DiNardi.

He couldn't get a real read on him, and this troubled Robert to no end. He liked the scholarship fund set up to help the less financially able, but he didn't like DiNardi's secrecy when it came to other parts of the school. He was aware that most of the scholarships were being given to highly talented athletes who would have normally ended up in the public school system. This really didn't keep Robert up at night because it led to St. Catherine's having one of the best high school football and hockey programs in the country. One of the last kids that Robert actually wrote a very generous tuition check for was a strapping mass of humanity named Stanley Antoine. Antoine, barring an unforeseeable catastrophe, would be recruited to a true football powerhouse and eventually play in the NFL. Robert also knew that it would be another notch in the St. Catherine athletic belt and more positive PR. Robert's philosophy was that if the kid came for football and received a world-class education, then wasn't it all worth it in the end? And if the kid grew up and played a professional sport, then maybe he would call them one day and get them on board to write an enormous check like he had done for them. Pay it forward or be made to look like a cheap, lackluster, ungrateful bastard.

It wasn't the athletes getting the tuition that bothered him; it was the academic part that vexed him beyond imagination. The fact that Robert usually had Thanksgiving dinner with the commissioner of the National Football League didn't hurt in getting checks from pro players, organizations, and their stakeholders. It also assured that Antoine and others who went before him would get drafted if things did not work out as planned.

Robert wanted St. Catherine's High School to be the academic epicenter of technology and advancement. He wished for his former school to harbor the great young minds of their generation and to cultivate their intellect in unimaginable ways. He felt thoroughly nourished intellectually while at the school, and he wanted both his money and his name to be attached to a school that developed the future Edison, Salk, or Carver. Robert knew how much was needed to achieve that, and that much of it was beyond his capacity. You can place money at the foot of a problem, but that does not create a solution.

He didn't know anything about hiring teachers, building curriculum, state testing, or all the little nuances of a classroom. Robert took a page out of his own internal corporate operations manual. Place an individual in charge who could get the job done, give them what they need, and hold them accountable for progress. Reward them and punish with impunity. So when the board of trustees met with him to finalize the hiring of Ralph DiNardi as principal, he demanded a private sit-down with DiNardi the day before. The meeting lasted the length of one cup of coffee, and it consisted of Robert doing almost all the talking. It ended with a handshake and Robert leaning in close to Ralph DiNardi's right ear.

"I am not a fan. *They*"—he said, purposely waving his index finger in an outward direction— "seem to think you are. I will give my vote of confidence to the board on your behalf. I will give you all the help and support that I can. I am a phone call away if you need anything that will make St. Catherine's the very best high school in the nation. But, Mr. DiNardi, if you fuck this up, not only will I make sure that you never work again, but you will be visited by one or maybe two men who will make certain that you live the remainder of your life in a great deal of pain."

With that, Robert stood up, put on his beige London Fog trench coat, and walked away. DiNardi, physically and mentally shaken, sat for two more hours contemplating whether he should keep his name in the running or go back to his desk at the mid-level public relations firm he was working for. Was Hanover serious? He had never encountered such a brazen display of incivility. The next morning, he woke up after a fitful sleep. He tended to his normal routine and drove to meet the board. As he sat across from the search committee members, he remembered why they had courted him in the first place. They wanted a man with business acumen, a person who could reenergize the school, holding onto the rich tradition while rebranding the school for the next generation of tech-savvy students. He was their first choice. DiNardi accepted their appointment as well as the generous guaranteed salary that went with it.

In doing so, he caught only a glimpse of the world he was entering into. He looked over at Robert Hanover, whose gaze never once broke from his. He could feel Hanover's eyes practically emitting a red beam similar to Superman in the old comic books, even when he looked away. He shook hands with all the board members, trying his hardest to lose Hanover in the small crowd that had amassed. He could feel the dry coolness of the sweat that had collected on his back during the meeting. DiNardi recovered his coat and made it to his car, feeling relatively calm and certain that Hanover had been joking about him being visited by two men. Hanover hadn't made a real attempt to see him after the appointment was confirmed. When he got to his car, he thought he saw what looked like a parking ticket under the windshield. He picked it up, realizing it was not a parking ticket at all. He opened it and felt an immediate need to vomit. On the nicest ivory stock stationery, he had ever felt existed two words printed in the neatest handwriting he had ever read: "Remember coffee."

What DiNardi didn't realize, nor could he realize at that time many years ago, was that note was not placed on his windshield by two hulking henchmen or two movie-type heavies who hired by Mr. Robert Hanover. It was placed there by a rather attractive, sophisticated-looking young woman who walked gracefully in extremely high heels that made her five-foot one frame rocket up to five-foot five. The young woman was a mix of Russian and Dutch, and she adopted both cultures in just the right physical way. After carrying out her assigned task, she walked down the block, adjusting her stylish, red-framed sunglasses. She reached into the small front pocket of her red leather Prada handbag and pulled out the keys to her BMW.

———◆———

WITH HIS PHONE IN HAND AND AN ACCELERATED heart rate Ralph DiNardi spoke with caution.

"Robert, we have a bit of a...issue that needs to be addressed."

"What kind of...issue?"

"Do you have time to sit down and meet?"

"No, I don't, but it seems I should, doesn't it?"

"For this...Yes."

"Thirty minutes then."

"Where?"

"Coffee."

CHAPTER 11

DiNARDI NEVER ENJOYED HIS CONVERSATIONS WITH Robert Hanover. They were always too long and extremely fraught with an indescribable anxiety, and he always ended up being convinced of something he didn't actually believe or made to feel stupid for not arriving at some simplistic answer that Hanover had already thought of. DiNardi could hold his own with most people he spoke with, but Hanover was unlike anyone he had ever met. He felt inadequate when speaking to him. It could have been the enormous wealth Hanover presided over. It could have been the business savvy and intelligence. It could be the looks. It could also be all fucking three of those things mixed with the fact that DiNardi was unbelievably terrified of Robert Hanover ever since the first conversation they had at this very same coffee shop several years ago when DiNardi was actually evaluated for the headmaster job at St. Catherine's. There was something about Robert Hanover that struck fear into him. He could not exactly place it mentally, and he had a difficult time even explaining it to himself. He saw Robert Hanover as a man who would go to absolutely any length to protect himself and his interests. He did not see him as a criminal or some elusive crime boss. He didn't see him as a murderer or anything as gratuitous as such. He might be wrong, and he hoped in a large way that he was completely mistaken; however, DiNardi felt that people who possessed the kinds of money that Hanover did must have soiled their hands at some point. Dirty hands create friction, and that friction usually helps to hold on to all the money.

DiNardi was by no means comfortable financially. He did have an excellent pension and retirement setup from his years in the private sector, doing the "corporate thing," as he called it. That would be kicking in when he turned sixty-five in five years. He also made a very nice salary as headmaster of St. Catherine's. There were also some "extracurricular" funds that assisted his bank account at certain points of the year. DiNardi made his money, but he was also in debt up to the wrinkles on his receding hairline. At last estimation, DiNardi's financial planner informed him that he and his wife, Linda, were approximately a half million dollars in debt. The approximation came about due to Linda's ability to habitually lie about what was owed, what was bought on credit, and what exactly was located in certain accounts. It had been a combination of living beyond their means, garish and ostentatious displays, and extravagant vacations. There were also the completely unnecessary purchases, such as twenty-five-thousand-dollar commissioned portraits of the two of them, which were lavishly framed and professionally hung in the even more ornately decorated entryway in their second home. The second home in the country was aside from the first in the city. Linda had to have the second home because it housed a small stable where she kept her competitive show horse, Rolex. The horse was an anniversary gift given to Linda from Ralph and, yes, it was named after the watch. It was named so because on the same anniversary that Linda received her horse, she had purchased a twenty-eight-thousand-dollar Rolex watch for her husband. The engraving on the back read, "Where does the time go? Happy Twenty-fifth." The DiNardis turned O. Henry's morality-inducing short story "The Gift of the Magi" into their own little garish love story on steroids.

What DiNardi truly felt was a sense of uncertainty when it came to Robert Hanover. What was he capable of, and just what would the fallout of the events of today be when he explained them over coffee? What did Hanover mean years before when he whispered a threat about taking his legs out? Was that a joke? An empty threat? An emasculating comment challenging his manhood? No matter what it was, he didn't like it, and he wished Cloughey, the root of all this bullshit, could just walk in front of a fucking moving bus or slip off a train platform. That would solve everything. Erasing Cloughey would make for the happiest ending of all. He had given the little bastard a chance to explain himself, and he just sat there staring into space as if he was above it all. DiNardi felt somewhat guilty about his bus and train thoughts but then neatly tucked them away and chalked it up to the day.

DiNardi stared out the window of Teresa's, a small coffeehouse close to campus. Teresa's was owned by Teresa Angilotti, a graduate of St. Catherine's and a loyal donor to the alumni fund. Teresa knew of all the comings and goings of St. Catherine's, and she was friendly with students, faculty, and staff. Her establishment was constantly full of rumors and coffee drinkers in need of a strong fix of Sumatra and an even stronger fix of tabloid. She knew DiNardi, and she gave him a smile and a few polite and obligatory words as she personally seated him at his small marble-topped table. DiNardi snapped out of his mini daze and thought about how pleasant Terry always was and how she was always smiling. He imagined working here rather than at St. Catherine's. Life would be so simple. Then, like a slap in the face with a cold, calloused hand, he focused sharply on something. *Why would Robert Hanover choose to meet me in the place where campus gossip gives birth?* He frantically began to pick up his coat and scarf when he heard a voice in front of him.

"I ordered you a double espresso."

DiNardi shifted his eyes upward to see Robert Hanover standing over him. As he removed his coat and pulled out his seat, DiNardi muttered something to his subconscious and screamed something ugly and vulgar inside his own head. The events of this day just evolved into something much worse than they already were.

CHAPTER 12

MICHAEL SAT ALONE AT HIS DESK IN THE OFFICE OF the English department. The office was usually a crowded place, given the twelve English teachers employed at St. Catherine's. That, mixed with the myriad of students who always seemed to wander in for whatever reason, made the English office one of the busier places on campus. Michael informed himself that this was no accident. Word had gotten out and spread quickly, and he was alone—a leper properly quarantined so that he couldn't contaminate any other healthy member of the community that was St. Catherine's College Preparatory School.

He sat with slouched shoulders and his head slightly drooped. His entire body was besieged by anxiety, and he felt himself running what was probably a mid-level fever. Lara had taught Michael how to breathe when he felt anxious: in through the nose, hold slightly, and then release slowly through the lips. That mixed with his medicine usually worked. It was not working today. He felt himself a puddle of sweat and confusion, and his dress shirt, once properly ironed and crisp with light starch, was a remnant of its former self. Above all, he felt nauseous and checked to measure the distance of the garbage pail to his chair, just in case.

In the Incredible Hulk comic books, a predictable formula always emerged. Some foolish contingency would attempt to contain, capture, or corner Dr. Bruce Banner in some way. Dr. Banner, feeling the anxiety of the moment, would try to fight it off, but inevitably, he would become the Hulk. The Incredible Hulk would then usually end up destroying everything and everyone in sight. He would run off to seek solitude and eventually wake up in the woods somewhere as Bruce once again. The only remnants left of his superhuman self were the ripped shirt and pants that were only held together by threads. Feeling alone and afraid, Banner would usually roam from town to town in search of not only a cure for his illness, but for some peace.

That is what Michael Cloughey longed for his entire life, peace. To be alone, left alone and free. His entire existence seemed confined, a consummate prisoner to no one and everything all at the same time. It was ironic, pathetic, and hypocritical all at the same time. He loved Lara and his son; he loved his brother. He even, for the most part, loved his job. How could he be so lucky to have these people in his life while simultaneously desiring to be free of all of them? It was the one and only secret he kept from Lara his entire life because if she knew he felt this way, she would be destroyed. He had destroyed enough with his hands; he didn't wish to invite his thoughts to the melee. He didn't want to be away from his family. He didn't want to take off and abandon them. His mind and his body were just demanding freedom. This feeling had burrowed itself deep into Michael at a very young age, and he had carried it with him his entire life. To endearingly love something or someone and want to be free of them simultaneously was a torment. Michael kept this mental contusion hidden.

People keep secrets. People tell lies. People save the feelings of others. People are myths, smoke. Michael Cloughey was all those things, and he did all those things, and if you called him on his shit or pushed him in some way, he pushed back to the point of making you sorry you had ever seen him. It was Sean who remarked one day that there was no greater punishment than his brother being born into the body he was. If he had been born into a frame of a six-foot, five-inch man weighing 280 pounds, perhaps every challenge, every glance, and every remark would not have felt like a threat, and they would be erased as easily as blackboard chalk. But Michael felt all those things were slights that challenged his manhood, his physicality, his intelligence, his balls. Michael turned his confinement and its mental imprisonment into ferocity. If you even attempted to cage the Hulk, he would smash until there was nothing left. Then he would leave. Well, Michael kept destroying and destroying, but he couldn't leave. There was a woman who gave her life and trust to him and a little boy who was expecting to play catch this afternoon in the backyard.

He went down to maintenance and got a large box and brought it up to his desk in the still enigmatically empty English department. He began to fill it with all the stuff people fill boxes with when they leave a place they have been at for a long time. When he was done, he repeated the task twice more, filling three large boxes in all. Every time he walked down the hallway, he caught the glances of the students and heard whispers emanating from corners. He felt fatigued by it all. He knew this was his last day at St. Catherine's, so he didn't bother to dwell on it. When he was done packing, he sat at his desk and waited for a call or an announcement or for someone to tell him the police had arrived to pick him up. Every time he thought about being taken away in handcuffs, he felt his stomach flip and he checked for the metal pail near his desk again.

By three o'clock, no one had called for him or checked on him. By 3:30 p.m., the parking lot on campus was as empty as it was when he had arrived that morning. By 3:45 p.m., the entire school felt like one of those bad horror films where the protagonist runs from the killer through the halls of a school or hospital late at night. Lights off and doors closed. St. Catherine's was usually a very active building, and the grounds of the school were usually ripe with activity. Track teams running, band practicing, choral group singing...

"Mr. Cloughey. Mr. Cloughey!"

"What!" Michael snapped his head up from his folded arms on his desk and looked up to see the face of the Vera Conroy, Ralph DiNardi's secretary.

"Well, I called, and you never answered, so I came up. "Are you ok?"

"Yes." The room was stifling. Michael rubbed his eyes and arched his back and neck in a tense and mildly satisfying stretch.

"You don't look well. Would you like me to get the nurse?"

"No. Thank you, Vera." Michael looked at his desk and ran his hands across it to find no boxes. All his belongings were still in their much too neat order on his desk. He looked at his watch and it read 1:43 p.m. It wasn't even a real sleep; it was a long fucking nap. He sat slouched.

Vera leaned down to meet Michael's drooped gaze with her eyes. She adjusted her glasses and read off a pink piece of telephone message pad that, by the looks of it, had been abruptly torn off. Michael knew for a certain fact that DiNardi's abrupt nature and utter lack of concern for those below his tax bracket scared the shit out of Vera. She read with purpose. "Mr. DiNardi called and told me to tell you to go home for the day. He and one of the board members of the school will be paying you a visit at home later this evening." Vera's speech was slow and deliberate, and she occasionally gestured with her hands as if she were providing inadequate sign language to the hearing impaired.

Michael looked up at her abruptly. "I can go home? Now?"

"Yes, sir." She nodded to confirm the message. "That's what he said to me to tell you. Are you sure you are all right? You look pale, and you're awfully sweaty."

"What else did he say?" Michael stood up and felt the room sway and his blood pressure drop. His head ached, and he stopped to close his eyes and regain his balance and focus.

"Nothing." Again, she read off the paper. "He just told me to escort you out through the delivery entrance and Not… the…front." She spoke the last three words with emphasis as if they had been told to her that way.

Michael leaned on his desk chair with both hands and stretched his eyes open. Vera Conroy was a sweet woman, a throwback to the days of secretaries before the term developed a slavish connotation and became administrative assistant. She had pride in her appearance and her work. Vera was never absent, never late, and she was extremely meticulous when it came to paperwork and numbers. Michael always envied individuals who were gifted in math and who could manipulate numbers like he could words and phrases.

Michael always stopped to ask her about her grandchildren and her husband, and he always remembered to bring her flowers or a card for the holidays. The other teachers usually threw her the obligatory "Hi" when they walked past her, but Michael saw her smile and blush one day when he handed her an extra coffee and croissant that he had gotten from the deli. It was a moment of genuine kindness, and she seemed thankful and very touched that someone saw her as a person, a human being and not a fossil. From then on, they became very friendly, her asking about his family and him asking about her dentist appointments or her arthritis flare-ups. He always tried to get her to call him Michael, but she could not bring herself to do so. She referred to everyone with a formal address of Mr. or Ms. She was pleasant, and she reminded him slightly of Yah with her overall temperament and considerate tone. At this moment, he was glad she was the first real form of human contact he had since he punched a student in the face. He felt guilty, but he just could not resist plying her for information.

"Any word from Stanley Antoine's parents? Are they here? Is everyone talking about me?"

Vera looked over her left shoulder at the small window in the door. Seeing no one, she leaned in toward Michael. She spoke in whispers. "Mr. Antoine took his son to the emergency room, and Mrs. Antoine is sitting with Mr. DiNardi in his office right now. They are in there with a board member, Mr. Hanover. You didn't hear any of that from me." She gave Michael an overexaggerated wink, knowing he would not betray the source of this information.

Michael smirked. "What else should I know?"

"Well, not much else to really report, Mr. Cloughey, except that Mr. DiNardi has your entire class in the waiting room outside his office. Kinda strange. All fifteen students, except poor Mr. Antoine, of course. They are just sitting there, looking nervous, not talking." She shrugged. "Are you well enough to leave?"

"Yes. Thank you, Vera." Michael put on his jacket, slung his brown leather messenger bag over his shoulder, and took a deep breath.

They walked in relative solitude down a side staircase and toward the delivery entrance where an assortment of boxes and packages lay about in disarray. When they got to the door, Vera stopped and said, "Good luck, Mr. Cloughey. I hope everything works out. My regards to your wife and son. Just call me if you need anything."

"Thank you so much, Vera. I do too. Please send William my best."

Vera offered a sincere yet subtle smile and closed the door behind him. He felt the early November air, crisp and invigorating, enter his nose and lungs. The sweat that at one point coated his body was now dry and somewhat sticky. He felt the need for a shower and shave. As Michael walked in, his customary head down, shoulders forward charge, he wondered why the police had not been called, why he was not sitting in an office being yelled at by this Mr. Hanover or Mrs. Antoine. Most of all, he was wondering why his entire class was sitting outside of DiNardi's office in silence. He did remember, thankfully and somewhat nostalgically, something his father had made mention of many years ago. If you truly want to know all the comings and goings in any business, you befriend two types of individuals, custodians, and secretaries.

CHAPTER 13

WHILE MICHAEL WAS NOT ENJOYING A POWER NAP, Ralph DiNardi was sitting in a café enjoying himself even less than he imagined he would be. After Hanover sat down, DiNardi carefully prepared his coffee for proper consumption by delicately adding skim milk in two increments and three packets of sugar individually. He sipped from his creation several times, stirred the hot coffee a few times, and tapped the stirrer on the top of the cup a few times.

"Do you want me to sit here a little longer until it's just perfect and pretend that my time doesn't fucking account for anything, or should I leave, and you can send me a fucking telegram?"

Sweat was building a small wading pool in DiNardi's underarms, and his forehead and upper lip resembled that of a man taking a steam bath. He did not want to make eye contact with Robert Hanover so he blurted out the first thing that came to mind.

"Your kid Antoine."

"What?"

"Antoine. Stanley Antoine. He -- "

"Fuck. Is he doing drugs? Did he get someone pregnant? Teenage boys are animals. They fuck everything. Who is she? That's what you called me for? Holy shit. You had me shitting on the ride over here. Ralph, what the fuck? You couldn't have gotten it done? These girls can't keep their legs closed when it comes to athletes." Hanover straightened the bottom flap of his jacket as if he were about to stand up and walk out.

"No. That's not it, Robert." DiNardi sighed and looked up. "A teacher…His English teacher punched him in the face this morning. In class. I am pretty sure his jaw is broken, and he is currently being taken to the hospital by his father. His mother is on the way to my office as we speak. To say she is angry would be sugarcoating the statement."

"Wait…what?…Antoine?…Stanley, the football and hock…?" Robert closed his eyes and then stared straight up at the ceiling as if something, a script perhaps, were written on it. He spread both hands apart and placed them on both corners of the table closest to him as if he were going to break the white marble in half. He looked at Ralph DiNardi and spoke in a very hushed manner.

"Okay. Ralph. You mean to tell me that Stanley Antoine, who is as big as a fucking grizzly bear, was punched in the face in school this morning by an English teacher? Who is this teacher? What is he, like, seven feet tall or something? Did Stanley threaten him or hit him first? Was it a self-defense thing? Jesus Christ, do you know what this means? Tell me the entire story as quickly as you can. Do not forget one thing." Robert took out his cell phone and dialed Anya. When she answered, he told her to say nothing and just listen. He immediately placed her on speakerphone.

Ralph was organized and specific and extremely detailed in his thoughts and his speech. He surprised himself. He thought he would come across as a bumbling idiot. He identified Michael Cloughey as the teacher who hit Antoine, and he gave a careful description of Cloughey. The description provoked Anya's only question, which she apologized for. "He's how big?" she asked. Robert made a circular motion with his hand as to progress the proceedings. DiNardi went on to explain the class and the parents and that he had already sequestered the class in his outer office after it happened. He repeated that he had done that immediately so word could not spread. He also bravely repeated that he had taken their cell phones as if he had cured some horrific disease.

Robert nodded at this retelling, and when Ralph stopped talking, he held up his hands and shrugged as if to ask if he was done. Ralph said, "Yes, that is all I can tell you as of now."

Robert picked up his phone, took it off speaker mode, and said, "Got it? Let's Ticonderoga this, vault the parents, and Milgram the spies." He hung up without saying anything else and put the phone in the inside pocket of his suit jacket.

Ralph DiNardi was relieved to have gotten all of this off his chest. He felt he had done right by Robert Hanover and that Hanover would now see that and they could solve this crisis as a team. He felt that he had impressed upon Robert that he was right for giving his approval to hire him as headmaster of St. Catherine's. He took a large swig from the mug of coffee before him, and even though he preferred tea, the contents of the cup soothed his dry mouth and lips. It was a rewarding drink. He narrowed his eyes at the brief conversation Hanover had with whoever was on the phone, and he asked who the person on the other end of the phone was.

Robert Hanover leaned in very closely, sighed, and clenched his jaw. He spoke through teeth and his gaze never broke with Ralph DiNardi's. "The person on the other end of the phone is the only person that can save your life right now, Ralph. If the person on the other end of the phone is not successful, you will be dealt with accordingly in forty-eight hours. No, I am not fucking with you. However, if the person on the other end of the phone is successful, you will live to speak at graduation. Either way, I would *not* yet book a vacation this summer. By the way, where is this fucking Cloughey right now?"

"I sent him home."

"You sent him…?" Robert uncrossed his legs and looked at his watch, a silver TAG Heuer Aviator with a royal blue oyster face. "If you make it past my forty-eight-hour deadline, I am going to explain to you just how much of an idiot you are and just how fucking incompetent you are. And then I am going to cut your balls off and make you sit in a corner with them in your hand while I fuck your ugly, shriveled-up wife in front of you. Get the fuck up. Let's go. By the way, what about the girl?""Not a word."

"She's smart. She'll be in Yale in six months."

CHAPTER 14

MICHAEL USUALLY TOOK THE TRAIN HOME, BUT HE was in no rush to see Lara. This was an unusual feeling for him because he normally couldn't wait to see her after work. All these years later, and he still not only desired Lara, but he still loved talking to her, making her laugh, watching her smile. This walk would serve its purpose to help him formulate an excuse as to how he had, in the course of one day, one morning, destroyed his life and perhaps their existence together.

The walk also calmed Michael down. He was convinced he was going to jail, so why not half-heartedly enjoy the weather before you are arrested and put in jail for ten years? Ironically, Michael wasn't sure how much time a person would get for assaulting another person, let alone a minor. He thought in approximations, and he guessed that he would do probably five to seven years. All the fights he had in his life, all the punches he threw, all the bones he broke and skin he cracked with his fists led to this. All those unpunished exercises of brutality got him to this day. Michael's parents did their share of talking and convincing when it came to Michael's attacks. When furious parents showed up at their door ready to have Michael arrested, the Clougheys would invite them in and persuade them to handle it all between themselves. Hours of bargaining and mediation, begging and coercion, crying and handshaking led to this walk home in November. Parents normally handled things among themselves when it came to their kids and their fighting. Fights between kids were nothing more than a thing that kids did. It was self-regulation and conflict resolution. Police were usually not alerted, lawyers were not called, and the legal system was not placed on alert if two kids threw haymakers at one another. It was a sort of justice that kids, especially boys, just doled out upon one another. It took a lot more nerve to look another kid in the face and scrap it out than to take out your cell phone and send a string of harassing and hate-filled text messages in the comfort of your bedroom. Nothing quite replaces looking another person in the eye when you are being cruel and demoralizing, and sometimes when you get it all out of your system and empty the tank, you oddly end up as friends, and that friendship would sometimes last years.

However, today was not in the same zip code as those childhood incidents. Who would litigate for Michael with this latest infraction? Virginia Cloughey was gone; she had been victimized by one of the most aggressive forms of cancer. Half of John Sr. sat on the mantel in Sean's room in a sealed porcelain jar. The other half had been thrown into the ocean at his request. This was not an event that you could "I'm sorry" your way out of. Even Dave Mantinakis's parents were convinced to let Michael off the hook back then when they were convinced by Michael's coach, during a closed-door one hour and almost forty-five-minute meeting, to let the family handle it all. The coach, by a stroke of pure luck, perhaps, was named Mitchell Trammell. He was Lara's father, and he eventually and with mixed emotion became Michael's father-in-law. It would be wonderful if Coach Trammell could fix this one with a quick hour-long peacekeeping summit. Mitchell Trammell had died of a heart attack two months after Lara gave birth to Mitchell's grandson.

No, there would be no one to solve this situation for Michael. He would not put this on his wife to solve or repair. It is the lowest thing to do to have your wife fix your holocausts. Lara had seen, heard, and felt almost every single one of her husband's fights throughout his life. She had made the emergency room visits, soaked the knuckles, prepared the ice packs, and washed all the bloodied clothes. Perhaps some would classify her as an enabler as well. Michael would rather flee the country than ask his wife for help today. Anyone that knew Michael Cloughey knew just how difficult it was for him to be without Lara. It was as if you were separating conjoined twins with your bare hands. Ever since that day when he spotted her at the park on the swings, Lara Trammell and Michael Cloughey had formed a bond that men, women, and children tried to pry apart, but Michael and Lara were so close that they made Bonnie and Clyde look like total strangers. John Sr. put it best when he told Sean one day that getting between those two was as difficult as "getting between the color green and money."

So as Michael walked, he mulled it over and thought about the only person he could call to help him through this colossal fuckfest. Michael had not spoken to Father Sean Cloughey since the day of his wedding, and that was only out of necessity.

Michael dug out his phone from his pants pocket and noticed that he had approximately a quarter of the battery left. He looked up his brother under his contacts. The sky was darkening with heavy, oddly shaped rain clouds that looked like a mix between boulders and trolls. At that moment, Michael started to feel slight rain trickles on his face and hands.

Great, he thought. *Even Stephen King couldn't foreshadow this phone call any better.*

Michael hated the rain ever since his childhood baseball days when valuable innings and games would be destroyed. It was no mistake that tears and raindrops looked awfully similar.

Attempting to avoid the rain, Michael ran under an awning in front of a tired-looking deli. He finished dialing. He took a deep breath and swallowed hard. The voice on the other end was stoic, monotone.

"Michael."

"Sean, I need to see you."

———

DURING CHILDHOOD, THE RELATIONSHIP BETWEEN brothers establishes itself. As the two brothers grow older, the relationship either solidifies itself or it becomes acquaintance based. Only children can't understand it because they are too busy pining for some form of comradeship. Kids in large families cannot understand it because they are too busy seeking out some form of solitude away from the massive amounts of activity in their home. The sister relationship is different because there comes a time when the brother becomes the protector figure and keeper of the peace regarding his sister's purity. Laertes and Fortinbras put it to Ophelia when the father and son duo threatened her to stay away from Hamlet if she wished to preserve the sanctity of the family name. Much good that did Ophelia as she was destroyed by her father, brother, and lover simultaneously. The brother relationship is one all its own. It should not be taken lightly, and it most definitely should not be interfered with. It is quite all right for one brother to beat the stuffing out of the other, but if an outsider were to attempt that indiscretion, it would make the Battle of Normandy look like a game of dodgeball.

THE CHILDHOOD FRIENDSHIP BETWEEN MICHAEL Cloughey and Lara Trammell went through its paces. The swings and their twosies partnership were a metaphor for the rest of their life together. At points, the swing was at its highest point and their friendship, life, and love was filled with excitement, anticipation, hysterical laughter, and dependence upon each other's presence. At its worst points, the relationship was at the bottom of its pendulum and the lows were, in a word, extensive.

They were truly two individuals who enjoyed each other's presence beyond belief. They shared a common sense of humor and a passion for what the other did. They reveled in the fact that what the other one did well they could not do at all. Jealousy was a stranger between them because they were both acutely aware that there was not an individual who could come between them. Those who tried met with Lara's tough-mindedness and a slap from her hefty intellectual hand. If that were not enough to dissuade the attempted wedge, then Michael would surely solidify the point with a more blunt and literal punch to some portion of the body that would offend in the most painful of ways.

Yah always believed the childhood relationship between her son and this little girl was a playtime phase. When it proceeded through puberty, John Sr. started to call Lara Michael's "Mrs." Most kids would be bothered by the ribbing and fatherly mocking, but Michael never was. Behind closed doors, John Sr. even told his wife that he believed Lara was the only individual on the planet who could actually put Michael in his place, both physically and mentally. John Sr. knew immediately that Lara was the best medicine for his son's "unique" disposition.

While in high school when most teens get their fill of each other and go their own ways, Michael and Lara became closer. They were inseparable, and they became obnoxious to those around them with their inside jokes and completing each other's sentences. Lara was talented in math and science, and Michael was a highly gifted writer and lover of history. Lara was a pianist and loved music, fashion, and design. Michael was the athlete who loved to be outdoors, especially on the baseball field. They seemed to naturally avoid the pitfall that plagues every couple at some point—they never attempted to change the other person. They accepted each other, scars, warts, bed hair, and all. While other teen couples were in flux and suffering from jealousy, gossip and "he said, she said," Michael and Lara were laughing and truly enjoying each other. Their friends and families could not understand the anomaly that was before them.

Michael Cloughey was not a saint. He did spend a portion of his youth chasing every attractive female, and he convinced many that sex with him was equivalent to seeing Jesus for the first time. He was successful in his exploits, and his name did get around. This didn't bother Lara Louise Trammell in the least because Lara Louise Trammell was unlike most if not every other woman that walked the earth that God made for us to put our feet upon.

The day that Lara laid eyes on little Michael Cloughey at the playground, she knew as a certainty that he would be her husband someday. Her parents had an amazing relationship, and she felt tremendous love and the overwhelming spirit of friendship that existed between them. When she would ask her mother who her best friend was, her response was always the same humorous yet truthful one: "that insane man who lives with us." When Lara asked her father the same question, he would make a crazy face, stick his tongue out, grab her, and say, "The lady in the house that drives me crazy." He and Lara would usually end up in hysterics due to this. She loved the fact that her father could break down the strong fatherly wall and just be silly. Her dad was a jokester, the eternal master of the prank. Mitchell Trammell loved to make jokes so that those around him would laugh, especially his little girl. The heartier the laugh, the better. The harder it was for you to catch your breath, the more satisfied he felt. When you are ten and your father uses a whoopie cushion at the dinner table, it leaves an indelible impression on the portion of your brain where memories reside.

The ideal model of Lara's life partner was established very early on in her development—a person who made you feel loved and safe and who had the ability to be so silly that you forgot your surroundings. The other outstanding characteristic that she adopted from her parent's marriage was that they were two of the best friends that anyone could be lucky enough to have. Lara knew and knew young just what made her happy. She didn't need to explore, search, or sow any kind of wild oats. Michael made her laugh uncontrollably, he cloaked her in love and attention, and he made her feel intensely safe. Michael's demeanor was alarming with every other person that surrounded him. However, Lara Trammell knew that Michael Cloughey would destroy anyone and anything that got in their way. While others were fearful, she was comforted in knowing that he would never lay a hand on her. As a kid, she found Michael's anger to be highly entertaining. As a teen, she found it alarming and worthy of address. However, no matter the age or the circumstance, Lara never feared Michael. Even that very ugly day on the baseball field that showed her the true underbelly of Michael's anger was not enough for her to call a time-out on their friendship or relationship. It disturbed her, but she also felt sad that her friend would do that and could do that to another human being. Her mother, her grandmother, her friends, and even her teachers stopped her at some point to give her what they all thought was heartfelt and most original life coaching on the matter. Lara gave them the due diligence and respect of listening. Externally she was calm and still, but internally she was twitching and scratching the skin off her arms while screaming, "That's not my Michael! That's your Michael, not Lara's!"

So Lara allowed this crazy boy, who she was certain to become her husband and eventually her child's father, to engage in the pursuit of his carnal desires. After all, the two never declared themselves a couple. They never stopped to solidify any relationship status. They never even exchanged the obligatory "I love you" that so many throw around and discard like used napkins. Nope, they were friends, and she was so certain, so confident that their future would rest together that she didn't care who he found himself inside of, on top of, or underneath. It was only sex and probably lousy sex at that. For a teenage Michael Cloughey who loved vagina more than a lawyer loves to hyperbolize, this was as if a pot of gold had been left on his front porch.

Then one day everything evolved and came together and found itself living out the legacy that had, up until that point, only lived in Lara's imagination. It was a Christmas Eve when both Lara and Michael were nineteen. Over the years, they developed the habit of spending time with each other's families, afternoons with the Trammells and dinners with the Clougheys or vice versa. The plan allowed for the satisfaction of both mothers, who would spend days preparing for and laboring over enormous meals. It also maximized the amount of time that both fathers got to spend with the other's partner. John Sr. adored Lara and made no effort to shroud that fact from anyone. Mitchell Trammell, from his years of coaching Michael, developed a bond with Michael. The relationship was built on trust in the very palpable but unspoken agreement that he would be Michael's sole supporter in the Trammell clan, and in return, Michael would never hurt his daughter in any way.

On this particular holiday, both Michael and Lara were taking the walk from her house to his when Michael spotted an unusual shape between two cars. Michael ran up to it immediately and leaned over it. Lara shied away. It appeared to her to be a dead body, lifeless and alone. The person or thing she was looking at over her shoulder was covered in layers of fabric, making it look oversized and quite massive. Michael was trying to find a head or a face in all the garments, but he could not find the beginning of any of the fabric. He kept screaming, "Hello! Hey!"

After what seemed like minutes of digging, both Lara and Michael realized that this mass of clothing was actually a woman. Michael uncovered her face and squatted down near the ground and pulled her onto the sidewalk. He unthinkingly sat in three-day-old dirty snow, slush, and general street filth and slid both of his arms underneath her. Lara sidled up to them slowly after realizing what he was doing. He checked for a pulse on the woman's wrist and her neck. He put his ear to the dirty and bloodied face and squinted as if wishing to hear her breathing and perhaps willing her to as well. Lara was right behind Michael now, and she was waving to passing cars to stop and help them.

Michael slapped the woman's face gently to get some response, any response. He pulled open her eyelids, but they only showed what looked like two deeply set eggs. Michael sprang up to his knees and screamed at Lara to call an ambulance. She immediately began to fish for her phone in her oversized bag. Michael yelled her name, took his phone out of his pocket, and tossed it at her feet. It scuttled across the ground like a bug, and she stopped it with her foot once she realized what it was. Michael began performing CPR on the woman, and Lara felt her hands, both cold and shaking, trying to manipulate the phone. Michael noticed an odd thought course through him. The only reason he knew how to perform any of this lifesaving stuff was because he learned it in his junior year of high school in Mr. Kozart's phys ed class. Kozart, with a class full of athletes, realized that the obligatory sit-ups and jumping jacks would do nothing to enhance the lives of these young men. He changed his course of action and taught his students things such as first aid, CPR, and how to treat injuries. A retired paramedic, Kozart went over CPR constantly with them. This was a surprise Kozart lesson in the middle of the street. The only difference was that this time it really mattered. As Michael performed compressions and did his breathing, Lara screamed out the street and the scenario into the phone.

After what seemed like hours but realistically only took seven minutes, the ambulance arrived, and Michael was pushed out of the way by the medical technicians. They rolled the woman sideways onto an orange board, placed elastic straps about her body to lock her onto the board, placed a white foam brace around her head and neck for support, and then they slid the board into the back of the truck. Michael ran up to Lara and grabbed his phone from her frozen hand and yelled at her, "Go home!"

She just stared at him. He grabbed her shoulders and leaned down to make eye contact. One door of the back of the ambulance was slammed closed.

"Lara, go! *Now!*" He pulled up the collar of her winter coat around her neck and sides of her face, and he wiped a tear from the side of her nose.

Michael jumped into the back of the ambulance and slammed the door closed before the paramedic could even ask him who he was. Lara was left her standing there cold and crying. Lara, usually the calm one who was able to process emotion and plan courses of action, stood rooted to the curb staring at the back of the ambulance. Her eyes were filled with tears and her nose was running. Her knit hat and the hair underneath it was askew and completely tousled. The turning of the ambulance about four blocks away snapped her out of her fugue state. She repeated Michael's demand to go home. She bent down and collected her bag, which felt too heavy and somewhat childish under the circumstances. She sniffled and wiped her eyes with the back of her hands. She never remembered walking home. All she remembered was walking into her front door and into the kitchen where her mother screamed for her father, who ended up catching her as she fell into his arms.

After Lara was propped upright on the couch by her father and she caught her breath, she spent several minutes yelling at her mother to calm down.

Her mother just kept screaming: "What did he do? What did he do, Lara? Jesus Christ, on Christmas? What did he do to you? I am calling his father."

She was able to eat a little bit and drink some tea, but even two hours later, she still felt as if her fingers and ears were frozen solid.

Three hours later, she was sufficiently able to stop the heavy hiccuping of sobs long enough to tell them all story of why she delivered herself to them the way she had and why Michael was not there with her. She was physically present, but she told the story from a recognizable distance. She had never seen anything like that. Her entire family sat there wide-eyed. Reacting more to Lara's emotional gestalt than the event itself, some covered their mouths, and some wiped away small tears of their own.

Michael arrived at her house a little before eleven that night. His eyes were circled in black, his clothes were wrinkled and stained, and the hair around his temples was matted with dried sweat. Michael sat and spoke to Lara as if he were reading from a television transcript. He was removed, earnest, and attempting to hold back a rage like the one that found him on top of Dave Mantinakis.

They believed she was thrown from a moving car. Her identification named her as Octavia Guzman. Earlier in the day, she had been seen drinking with several men at a small lounge in the city. Much of that information was obtained by police by a pure stroke of luck. They found a small cocktail napkin in her pocket with chewed gum in the middle of it. The imprint and logo on the napkin led them to the lounge itself where the bartender and a bouncer claimed to have vaguely remembered her leaving with what they thought were two gentlemen. An even larger majority of what occurred from then until when Michael began CPR on her was still unknown. No one had reported Octavia missing. No one responded to any calls, and no one came to the hospital to see if anyone who fit her description had been brought in. When the doctors took off the packing and moving blankets that she was wrapped in, they found a rather small woman who had been beaten badly and stabbed twice. They said she was dressed as if she was perhaps going somewhere for the holiday. Michael didn't know where that was, but he really wanted to find out and there was a growing need in him to "get in contact" with the gentlemen who threw her from their car. This was where the paramedic shook Michael's hand and thanked him for doing what he did. The paramedic looked at his watch for a second, and Michael felt it coming. Olivia Guzman was pronounced deceased at 9:48 p.m. on Christmas Eve.

When he was done speaking, he looked up at Lara with eyes that were imploring him to release the tears he had been holding in all night. He didn't know how someone could treat another human being like this. He had seen murder on television and in film, but this was as if it were delivered to your front door. He felt and questioned every emotion that was striking him in the stomach and head. A part of him wanted to find these guys and destroy them in ways too terrible to even say to himself. Another part of him questioned why he was feeling such a catharsis for an individual he never even met or spoken to. Yet another side of him felt as if he let this woman down when he could not save her or at least add a few minutes to her evaporating existence. Most of all, he just hurt all over. His body and his head felt as if someone had spent the better portion of the night wrestling with him.

It was this day, this night, this experience, and these tears that acted as the delineating moment in Lara and Michael's young life. Sean would say that his brother and sister-in-law fell in love the moment they saw each other at the park as kids. It would be a point of contention between the two brothers for the rest of their relationship. However, for Lara Trammell, this was the day she mentally became Lara Cloughey. All the wasted time she spent truly committing to her feelings for Michael ended on that Christmas Eve. She never fully realized the fact that she loved him. She always knew she would end up with him because they couldn't stand to be away from one another. However, this night and what they shared created in Lara a desire to want to never be away from Michael, not even by accident. Some would argue that it was the stress of what they experienced that day. Some would say she saw a side of Michael that no one had ever seen. Some would say she just felt sorry for Michael because he looked so distraught over that woman's murder. Virginia Cloughey knew exactly what Lara felt and exactly why she felt it. Lara and Virginia did not see the kid who was capable of doing what he did to an opponent on a baseball field or the kid who was able to beat his brother into stitches the way he did for insulting Lara. Virginia and Lara both saw the little boy who, without prompting, brought the groceries in for his elderly next-door neighbor. The little boy who refused to take an offered folded-up dollar bill for the assistance. The little boy who held the door a lengthy amount of time for the elderly woman while she climbed the stairs to go inside. The little boy with the tousled hair that the old woman rubbed as she thanked him repeatedly. The little boy who went on throwing his ball up in the air afterward as if it never even happened.

Lara put her hand on Michael's and looked at him and told him that she loved him. She told him that he was the bravest person she had ever known and that, if it was okay with him, she would really love it if he would let her spend the rest of her life with him. Michael looked down and nodded.

Lara was fully aware of Michael's deep internal desire for righting what he felt were the wrongs around him or to those he cared for and loved. She never feared him, just what he could become at times. She knelt in front of him and grabbed both sides of his face and pried his head up so she could look into his exhausted eyes that were straining to stay open.

"Promise me that you will not do anything about this, Michael. Promise."

He nodded heavily again but said nothing.

"Fuck you. I said promise me, Michael Cloughey."

Michael took a deep breath and straightened up and looked up at the ceiling as to extend his burdened neck. When his heavy head and his neck returned to meet the level of Lara's, he opened his eyes wide and stared into her eyes so hard he swore he would exit on the other side.

"I promise."

He always kept that promise.

CHAPTER 16

Robert Hanover stood before Michael Cloughey's senior advanced English honors class, all except a one Stanley Antoine. The students had been told to line up their phones on Principal DiNardi's desk the moment they were brought in. DiNardi said nothing and rooted his eyes to the top of his desk. Their only deviation was the back wall of the office. He avoided any form of eye contact and left this meeting to the man standing on his right. Hanover spoke with a slow purpose, and his voice was distinct and unwavering. The words flowed as if he were reading a well-rehearsed script. Hanover even put in the inflection and gesticulations as if he were a well-practiced stage actor. His clarity was aimed at each one as if to scream, "I will say this once and there will be no follow up questioning." The students, all the brightest that the school would put forth to some of the finest universities in the country, sat with a focus and a purpose. Some were angry that they were made to sit there, some were confused as to what all of it meant, and others absolutely couldn't care less as to what this man had to say. No matter what their sentiment was, not one of them dared to express anything.

"You are here because of your English teacher, Mr. Cloughey. Today, before you, he brutally punched one of your classmates in the face. That classmate is currently at the emergency room being attended to. You are here and have been here for some time now, and Mr. DiNardi apologizes for this. You will be dismissed in a few minutes. You are thanked for your time and patience. Understand that this unfortunate set of circumstances has already happened, and there is absolutely nothing that can be done about it. No conversation, email, social network entry, or gossip session can make it vanish. You are the only students who know that this has occurred, and it will remain that way. I am here to tell you that the events of today go no further than this room and those in it. To speak of this event would be to destroy the tradition of excellence that this school views as absolute legacy. Those who have walked before you and those who will walk here after you rely upon to keep today to yourself."

Robert Hanover paused to take a deep breath and check his phone, which had been buzzing to indicate a text message. The texts were from his assistant. He returned his phone to his monogrammed brown leather Louis Vuitton phone case, a recent gift from his wife.

"For those of you who are not plugged into the historical aspect of what lies before you, I offer you this conciliatory proposal. If I hear that any of you have uttered even a word of this to anyone, I will see to it that you will find it impossible to gain admission to even a community college. I will work tirelessly to assure that your academic and occupational futures will be met with an absurd amount of resistance and struggle. If that is not enough, I will also see to it that recommendations you have received and any applications you have submitted vanish. I cannot make it any clearer than what I have just placed before you. I know you must have many questions. I know you may have numerous concerns. I am certain that you have many thoughts, feelings, and very principled ideals that the events of this morning have truly compromised. It is not as if I am unaware of these things. It is not as if I am ignorant as to what happened today. It's just that I simply don't care about any of your feelings and thoughts and ideas and collectively, my time is drastically more important than yours."

He paused here to be sure he locked eyes briefly with every single young person in the room. Robert Hanover was incredibly adept at saying very powerful things with his eyes alone. He wanted them to know he was threatening them, and he wanted them to be aware that he would recognize them should he see them again, anywhere, at any time. The silence in the room was suddenly and solely disturbed by the air purifier that DiNardi had on a timer to begin periodically throughout the day. The low hum was faint as if it were apologizing for disturbing Robert Hanover's lesson in intimidation.

"At this point, you are to collect your phones and depart. They have been wiped clean. You are dismissed."

All the students, except for one, did as instructed. She waited for the other students to leave, and she quietly and somewhat frightfully walked up to DiNardi's desk. She picked up her phone and stood looking at her principal.

"Yes, Nia. May I help you?"

"I don't blame Mr. Cloughey for what he did."

"What? Why would you say that?"

"Stanley had been on Mr. Cloughey for months now. Failing English last quarter got Stanley suspended from the team. He was supposed to get a visit from a scout to see him play, and when he was forbidden to play, they passed him by. He was so angry at Mr. Cloughey. He has been pushing his buttons for the longest time now."

"What exactly are you saying, Nia?"

"I am saying that if Stanley had not gotten suspended, none of this would have occurred."

"So you are defending your teacher for breaking a student's jaw, or are you blaming him for failing a student?"

"Stanley did everything he could to get under Mr. Cloughey's skin. He called him names, he threw things at him in class, and he even keyed the entire side of his car one time."

"In that case, why did Mr. Cloughey choose today to do what he did? Why not tell anyone? Why not speak to anyone about all of this mess?"

Robert Hanover focused on the young woman and peered at her profile as she spoke. She was a small in stature with very soft features. She had a rigid posture to her stance, and while she was addressing DiNardi, she made her case while maintaining eye contact. She possessed a sophistication in her demeanor that Hanover could not exactly place. He was not sure if she appeared older than her age or if she had been raised by parents who informed her that the giggly teenage girls who interject the word "like" in their vernacular every five seconds very rarely made a name for themselves. He was highly impressed with her poise and her speech. *She is going to do very well at Yale*, he thought.

Nia continued, "Mr. Cloughey spoke to Stanley privately. He knew that the scouts for the junior hockey traveling teams started coming around next month. That is a truly remarkable opportunity. He told Stanley that if he got his sh—his act together, that he would help him pass, perhaps even tutor him a bit."

DiNardi felt like the fourth smartest person in the room of only three people at this point. "It sounds as though Mr. Cloughey was trying to help Stanley. I am failing to see how all of that arrives us at this morning."

"When Mr. Cloughey spoke to Stanley that day, Stanley got really angry. He felt that Mr. Cloughey was overstepping his bounds and patronizing him. He had done some research on Mr. Cloughey. He said something like 'I don't need your help. You're a has been, a fucking wannabe baseball player who never got his shot.'"

"Nia, I really don't want you involved in all of this. Your future is remarkably bright. You don't need to speak for Stanley or Mr. Cloughey."

"I know I don't have to say anything, but, I mean, it's really strange because that day Stanley said that to Mr. Cloughey, he got up in his face and had his finger in Mr. Cloughey's chest." She walked up to DiNardi and mimicked the action with her right index finger.

Hanover interjected, knowing he had to get in touch with Anya immediately. "Land the plane please, Nia. I respect your sentiments here, but why is all of this so strange?" He leaned forward and tilted his head to the side as if to lower his eye level and thus will the clarity out of her.

"It is strange because when Stanley got up in Mr. Cloughey's face, all he did was turn around and walk away. He said and did nothing." She paused and looked at both men. Her arms were open slightly and her palms were turned upward to face the ceiling, thus emphasizing her point. "Today, however, it was all very different. Mr. Cloughey was walking around the room while we were taking a test, and when he got to Stanley's desk, Stanley turned his phone over to the screen side so Mr. Cloughey would see it. Mr. Cloughey took the phone and looked closely at it. He put the phone screen-side down on the desk and punched Stanley right in the face."

She stated the next portion of her recollection as if she were reading from the student handbook. "School policy states that while testing, in any capacity, all cell phones are to either be stored away, powered down, or kept screen-down until such time as the last exam has been collected by the teacher."

She took a slight breath only to get her last question out. "Why would Stanley show Mr. Cloughey his phone, Mr. DiNardi?"

"What was said? What was on the phone?"

"Absolutely nothing was said, and I have no idea what was on that phone. But I will tell you that I never saw Mr. Cloughey look like that. I have never seen *anyone* get like he got. It was unbelievably terrifying and then it was…just…well, over."

Hanover stood up straight and adjusted his tie and collar. "Thank you very much, Nia. We can handle all of this from this point moving forward. Please tell your parents Mr. Hanover said hello."

Nia picked up her phone from DiNardi's desk and slung her bag onto her right shoulder. "You're welcome. I will pass on your regards, Mr. Hanover." She turned to leave, and as she placed her hand on the doorknob, she was interrupted.

"By the way, is there any way you might be able to get your hands on your brother's phone?" Hanover asked probingly.

Nia Antoine turned and offered up a slight smirk. "I could try, Mr. Hanover, but that boy never lets that phone out of his sight."

"Well, if you can, you call me directly. Understand?" Hanover said as he stared directly into her sincere hazel eyes as he handed her his business card.

"I understand."

Five minutes later, Robert Hanover was outside trying to avoid getting his rather expensive leather shoes wet in the rain. As he approached his car, Hanover picked up his phone and dialed.

"Anya."

"Everyone has been called."

"Thank you. Before you leave, send me the cell numbers of both the Antoine twins as well as their parents."

CHAPTER 17

OF ALL THE PEOPLE IN MICHAEL'S UNIVERSE, IT WAS Sean who had witnessed, heard, and felt the brunt of almost every one of Michael's departures from civilization. The Christmas morning after the Octavia Guzman incident, Sean and Michael spoke at great length about the whole night. Above all things, Michael mentioned how bad he felt for this woman who had been discarded and thrown out like so much trash. He told Sean of his promise to Lara and Sean said it was a noble one. Sean said that what Michael did was heroic. Sean was a master at giving a compliment but disguising it with an inflection as if he were reading from a shopping list filled with the most unpleasant items on it.

Michael explained just how much hatred and rage he felt. It was going to be with him for a long time. He then went on and explained how Lara had forced him to make a ridiculous promise to not doing anything about it. He told Sean that he needed to do something and find the people responsible for killing her. He desired to have them feel the same pain he was sure she did. It was this conversation, held at the Cloughey dining room table over two nondescript sandwiches, one salad, and three oatmeal cookies, that acted as the railroad spike between the two brothers.

"In all honesty, why don't you just let the police handle it? You did a lot, and you just feel bad that this happened. Why compound matters with your usual antics, Michael?"

"You weren't there, Sean. You didn't see what they did to this woman. By the way, what antics are you referring to?"

"You know what I mean, Michael. You do these things. You do something good or noble and then you turn it into your own cause, and it becomes a bit of an event. You do this." He emphasized the wording of the last sentence as if to ask the question, "Are you new here?"

"I get carried away sometimes, but you make it sound as though I have a problem, Sean. The guys that did that are just supposed to get away with doing something like that to a woman? I'm supposed to just sit here and not get upset and frustrated and angry? I have not done this my whole life. What the fuck, Sean?"

"Michael, I'm your brother. I love you, but you have a problem. You feel like it's—"

"Now I have fucking problems. This is like you...to turn...I tried to save her, and Lara saw it and I just..."

"Stop getting all excited, Michael. I am trying to talk to you. Talk to you. And you are getting angry and—"

Michael slammed his fist on the table and leaned forward. "I'm getting fucking angry because I wanted to talk to you about this, and it all boils down to me having problems. And according to you I have had them…forever. How did this get where it is right now?"

"Michael, if you would listen for a few minutes, you could hear me out and—"

"And I could hear you tell me I have problems. I do not have fucking problems, Sean. You, you have fucking problems."

"Michael, I—"

"No. You know what…I just wanted to talk to you about this, and it's all fucked up now. Did you ever analyze yourself, Sean? Did you ever ask yourself questions? The fact that you can't seem to give a shit about anyone but yourself. A great fucking priest…You're perfect."

Sean sat back to create distance from his brother and his growing rage. "How can you say that? I have been here for you your entire life. I have always tried to…I know we haven't always been very close, but I have always tried to—"

"To what? *Save* me? You're the hand of God now, saving your little brother with 'problems'? Does it feel good, or do you feel like a failure because to you I am so fucked up? You're the one who doesn't have anyone in their life. All you do is sit at home and do nothing with no one. I have Lara. I have friends. I have always had friends. Lara told me she loves me, and you know what, I know I fucked around a lot, but I really do love her. A real love. I always have. It feels incredible to have someone. Has anyone ever told you they loved you, Sean? Anyone? Girl or Guy? You think I never thought about that? You think I never thought about your…preferences, your…inclinations? Who the fuck cares? Are you afraid to say it out loud or something? What is it, Sean? You like little boys or something? Ever since I was young, I…"

At this point in the conversation, Sean started to wonder where he was and what he was doing sitting across from this person. This could not be his brother. But unfortunately it was. He was prepared for this conversation. He had thought for years about what would happen the day they shared this specific dialogue, exchanged these words. In his head, the setting was different. The time would be different, and it would perhaps have gone slightly differently. However, it wasn't different. It was what it was, and it was happening right now, and he had a choice. He could let Michael explode and run out of gas. This would mean sitting here and accepting his brother's angry barbs and perhaps whatever came after those. The second choice was to finally just have the conversation that had been evolving for decades. The conversation that his father and mother avoided and were too parentally afraid to have. The conversation that everyone in Michael Cloughey's life just feared like a terminal illness. He knew that no matter which decision he made, it would result in his brother's hatred of him and perhaps a brutal retaliation. Would you rather be stabbed repeatedly or shot several times? This was ultimately the question. The result of all of this would be unbearable, and wasn't it a damn shame that he inherited this, all of this, from John and Virginia? Sean looked down at the knife next to the mustard and the fork that was next to his salad. He chose the fork.

He grabbed the fork with his left hand, which was slippery with sweat, and he jumped to his feet. Sean reached across the table and did what was owed to his brother from decades of eggshell walking. With his right hand, he reached across the oval kitchen table and grabbed Michael by his shirt. He pulled Michael toward him and met his face with the pronged end of the fork. Michael was spinning and for a moment lost all sense of where he was and what was happening. He was off-balance, and he was compromised to say the least. The chair he was sitting in had pinned his legs in a hyperextended fashion, and the table edge was now pressing into his upper midsection. Michael's arms were held under the table with the force of Sean's strength pulling him toward him, and his face was pressed to the cold wood of the table itself. Underneath him lay a cross section of the food on the table.

Sean could not believe he had been able to position his brother in a fashion that rendered him so helpless. He had thought about what would have happened had he missed grabbing him the right way. He feared what would have happened if he had missed completely or if Michael were able to get away completely. He told himself that his success was an indication that this event should and must happen at this moment in both of their lives. There did reside the small thought that he had just been incredibly lucky. Whether the event was a product of luck or fate, the Cloughey brothers were sharing this moment on the same table they shared many of their mother's delicious meals and their father's endless rants ranging from politics to sports to how he would just love it if the city would actually ever use his tax dollars to fix the roads and clean up the streets.

Michael could not believe that his brother was doing this. He could not believe that what seemed like an innocent conversation almost thirty minutes ago led to his brother attacking him as if they were inmates in a prison cafeteria. However, what had Michael most intrigued was just how strong his brother really was. He had never seen Sean in this way. He never knew Sean was capable of this kind of action. He also realized that Sean was much stronger than he was and how this strength was concealed from those around him.

"Listen to me, you little fuck. I should have put this to you a long time ago. It's my turn to speak and your turn to be spoken to. Your father should have done this years ago when you broke my face. You have been a problem ever since you were a kid, and someday you will probably kill someone. I am surprised you haven't already. Only Christ knows how it is you managed to stay out of jail this long. If it weren't for our mother constantly begging everyone to give you another chance, you would be there right now. Who told you it was okay to settle every little score and unfairness in this world with your fists? Every time someone disagrees with you or does something you think is unjust, you attack them. How does it feel? How does it feel to know that if you move, I could shove this thing right through your cheek? Try explaining that to the emergency room the way Ma had to explain my face when we were kids. What you did for that woman the other day was amazing, Michael, but why does it have to go past that? Just let it go. Let the police take it."

Michael said nothing, but he squirmed slightly as if to test Sean's mettle and the grip of his hands. Both were, without question, as much up to the task as the cutlery.

"Don't move and don't say anything. If you're even remotely intelligent, you will let this thing die, and if you're even slightly intelligent, you will run over to Lara's house right now and tell her to forget all about you. Tell her to find someone who probably won't end up in jail or possibly kill her someday over a stupid disagreement. If you really care for that girl and her family, who hates you by the way, you will let her go and be happy and you can live your angry, sad, and vile life all by yourself. Forget me. Forget I'm your brother and get the fuck out of here. I didn't choose you. We didn't choose each other. We have been stuck together from the day you were born. Go and tell that girl that you can't be with her. You owe her that. Then leave."

Sean released his grip and threw Michael backward as he stood upright and wiped his face with the back of his shirtsleeve. He was breathing heavily, and his heart was beating an elaborate metronome. Still holding the fork tightly, he sat back into his chair. Sean's hands were throbbing from clutching onto the fork and Michael's shirt. He put the fork down and placed a hand on top of it. He took his other hand and covered both of his eyes. He took a deep breath. It was more to suppress crying than it was to catch his breath.

Michael pulled his chair upright and sat down. He was completely covered in sweat, and his shirt was misshapen and slightly torn near the collar. Much of the food that was on the table was either on the floor or on Michael's shirt. His shirt resembled a kindergarten finger painting. He sat slouched with both palms on the table. His eyes looked to the tabletop where his body had just been turned into a tablecloth. His breathing was rapid, and he felt nauseous. Michael always suspected that his brother did not like him. He knew that Sean did not feel comfortable around him, but it was not until that night that Michael realized just how much his brother detested him.

Sean took a deep breath in and out through his nostrils and spoke softly with a level of composure that Michael could not summon at that point. His entire body was a knot, and he, too, felt queasy. The food, smeared all over the table and floor, did not help in this regard. With his head propped up by his right hand and his left hand still on top of the fork, Sean looked down as to avoid any form of eye contact.

"If you choose to marry Lara, I will be the one to preside over the ceremony. My commitment tells me I must. I am really hoping you decide to free her and go. The only thing I can tell you for sure, Michael, is that whatever your decision is, understand that you and I will never speak again."

CHAPTER 18

ROBERT HANOVER WALKED INTO HIS OFFICE AND closed the door behind him. He had just walked past Anya and said the word "ten" with a face that looked as if a puppy had been dropped from a building. Anya knew this meant he needed ten minutes to collect himself. Anya, without telling him, always gave him an extra five. He knew that, but he didn't want her to know he did. He liked that she did something small like that to protect him and watch over him. Hanover was not a man who slept long periods of time at night. He was always keeping track of various markets, getting calls at odd times from constituents, and of course tending to the occasional need or whim of a mistress. So the forced power nap served him well. Anya, for her own mental well-being, insisted Robert take a nap every so often. It gave her a much-needed break, and it made her boss much less ornery. One day Anya explained her job to her mother, and her mother said, "You went to college for this? You sound like the guy's wife." Anya laughed off her mother's sarcasm; however, the longer she worked for Robert Hanover, the more she realized she behaved like his mother. She was not above arranging naps, ordering healthy lunches, making up little white lies, and, upon occasion, going the extra distance to make sure a job was "tucked in and fast asleep" (completed with no chance of problems). When you balanced it all out, Robert needed her just as much as she enjoyed the pace he set and the acuity it took to get it all done. She was not spotless regarding the business and personal affairs of her boss. However, she knew for a fact that there were others who were involved much more profoundly than she.

Robert placed his coat in his office closet, went into the bathroom, and washed his hands and face. He removed his cuff links, rolled up his sleeves, and unfastened his tie halfway. He felt as though this were the first few minutes of the day that he had nothing going on. He was correct, but his availability would be short-lived. Stopping by his office refrigerator, he opened it and removed a bottle of Voss water and opened it. He felt the need to wash out his mouth from the bitter coffee he drank earlier and the conversation he shared with Ralph DiNardi. He was sick of DiNardi and the Antoine family and this Michael Cloughey individual who was at liberty to destroy all the efforts he and many other powerful men had created and even continue to create.

Hanover placed his water on the corner of his desk. Ironically, he happened to notice during his time in DiNardi's office that his desk was comparatively much more utilitarian than DiNardi's. This thought both aggravated him and sickened him at the same time. He wrote a note on his desk calendar to tell Anya to buy him new office furniture. It was either that or have DiNardi killed. He ambled over to his leather sofa and pulled off his shoes before lying back and closing his eyes. He was usually a heavy sleeper who could fall quickly into REM sleep once he had eliminated the ambient sound. He wondered who Cloughey was and what he was all about. To know a man was to know his value system. To truly know a man was to know just how far you could compromise his value system. This was true in two fields: politics and business. When it came down to it, politics was business wearing a dress, the phony democratic feel that appealed to the masses who thought that the real power players gave a shit and a half about the common working man. It was taboo to say it out loud, but he often wanted to scream at being surrounded by the middle to lower classes. It made his skin crawl how a human could live check to check, counting their change, cutting coupons, hoping for sales, budgeting, and, worst of all, eating leftovers. Jesus Christ, what a travesty. He understood how these proclivities would play to anyone outside of his own mind, so he kept them to himself and hid, as best as he could, the cringing and bitter scowls when faced with all of it.

Just how far did this Cloughey go today? What kind of guy was he? DiNardi told him he was a highly regarded teacher, a family man, a former standout athlete. How did he end up teaching at this school? Why would someone this vanilla and trite decide to violently punch a kid in the jaw? If Nia's account was true, then there was something on her brother's phone that would answer this question and probably tell a hell of a lot more about this guy. He had to squash this and squash it quickly. If anyone—a reporter or a detective, anyone—came digging in the dirt at St. Catherine's, they would find a hell of a lot more than worms.

Hanover cleared his thoughts and decided to just rest for a few minutes and process all this shit while he slept.

Exactly twenty-two minutes later, he was being nudged gently. As he began coming out of a rather restful nap, he heard a voice that was slow and cloudy. As he awoke, it became clearer and more identifiable. It was Anya. She was standing at his side nudging his shoulder. He opened his eyes wide as if to gain instant focus. Eventually her face was clearly before him.

"Mr. Hanover."

"Yes."

"Line two for you."

"Jesus, who is it?"

"Nia Antoine? She said she has what you are looking for?"

He sprang up off the sofa and immediately felt a rush come into his head, making him both dizzy and disoriented. He sat in the chair behind his now disappointing desk and picked up the receiver.

"Nia. Hello. This is Mr. Hanover. Robert. Thank you so much for calling. Could you hold for one second, dear? Thank you so much."

Hanover held the receiver to his chest and ripped off the piece of his desk calendar that held the note about his furniture. He handed it to Anya.

"You want me to kill Ralph DiNardi? Can't we just fire him?"

"Not that part, Anya. Under it."

She read it and looked at him with a crinkled face that suggested confusion. "What do we do with this furniture?"

"I don't give a shit."

He placed the receiver to his ear. "Okay, Nia, here is what I need you to do."

CHAPTER 19

"Sean, I fucked everything up today. I have no idea who to turn to, and I absolutely cannot speak to Lara about any of it. I just need someone to help me out here."

"Michael, I thought we agreed—"

"I know, Sean, I just—"

"I don't think we should—"

"I hit a student." Michael sighed deeply and released a long breath. "You were right, Sean."

"Where are you?"

"I went to buy some baseball cards."

"Stay there. I'll pick you up. Do not go anywhere."

CHAPTER 20

EDELBERTO PENA WAS THE OWNER AND STILL VERY
proud operator of Ponce's Deli and Candy Store. He was known
to his friends and to the frequent patrons as Berto. He was a
man that, at the age of eighty-four, could still sit down and be
more than willing to discuss his three favorite things. Having
owned his store for well over fifty years just about made everybody a frequent patron of Ponce's, and no one enjoyed taking
care of everyone from the neighborhood like Berto. The store
derived its name from his hometown in Puerto Rico. Ponce's
was a place where you could get seemingly everything from a
coffee and the paper all the way to completing a medium-sized
shopping list. John Sr. liked the store because Berto was the only
one in the neighborhood who stocked *The Irish Echo* newspaper, a staple in the Irish community. This fact prompted John
Sr. to turn Edelberto's name into "Eddie," short for Edward, a
proper Irish name. This was a name that stuck with the entire

family, and it would not be uncommon to hear the phrase, "Go to Eddie's and get…" The end of that sentence would be completed with a multitude of items such as bread, milk, cheese, etc. It would also not be uncommon if either Sean or Michael would be sent to pick up homemade chicken soup and cough syrup for the other during the more difficult cold and flu seasons. Virginia liked the store because Eddie allowed her to put stuff on credit, buying her some time to shop until John Sr. arrived home with his paycheck. At some points, the bill became rather too large to handle in one payment, but that was okay with Eddie. He felt that he was doing the predominantly blue-collar neighborhood a service. Because of his trusted ties to the neighborhood, Eddie became a sort of unofficial mayor, and he was provided with a decent amount of family squabbles, divorce stories, affairs, and birth announcements, and he even loaned out money to those in need of help from time to time. Ponce's Deli was a good thing for the neighborhood and for all of those who knew Edelberto Berto Eddie Pena. He loved his customers and his store. He loved taking care of his neighbors. He loved being there for people. Lucille, his wife, would get angry at times and then laugh at her husband at other times.

"*Pendejo*," she would say as she would ask him how much he would allow some people in the neighborhood to put on credit. Lucille knew that they stood a very large chance of never seeing that money collected. There were points, however, when she would sit out front and laugh when her husband was heard telling jokes to someone who just stopped in for a pack of cigarettes. A quick stop at Ponce's sometimes turned into two or three hours as Eddie would be willing to tell jokes, talk about politics, or discuss what he felt was the disregard and lack of appreciation of his beloved island of Puerto Rico.

Eddie felt that the overall contribution of the artists and writers of Puerto Rico was something that he could make up for if he explained it to enough people. He also felt that there was no finer overall player in the history of baseball than Roberto Clemente. Although he sincerely appreciated the contributions of Jackie Robinson, he felt disheartened by the fact that Roberto Clemente was never truly given the credit he deserved as an athlete and humanitarian. He once told a customer that when he was a younger man in Puerto Rico, he had stopped to watch Clemente hit a ball so far that he was able to pick up his glove, run, and catch it himself. "No man was the perfect combination of speed and power and agility as Roberto Clemente."

Lucille would laugh when he told this story and respond with a muttered, "*Estas loco.*"

The only family and individual that was exempt from Lucille's despair about their credit was the Cloughey family. Lucille loved Virginia like a sister, and the two became the closest of friends. John Sr. and Eddie would play dominoes, a game Eddie taught John Sr., on a small card table outside of the store on the weekends. It was during this time that a debate over the merits of Roberto Clemente versus Ted Williams would ensue. Williams was sainted by John Cloughey Sr., and in his eyes, Williams could do nothing wrong. Watching the "Splendid Splinter" play was equivalent to receiving an inheritance that you just knew was coming your way, and his swing was a gift from God. Most of the time, Eddie responded with a phrase in Spanish that would elude John Sr. In return, John Sr. would respond with "If you had anything worthy of saying, you would say it in English, my friend."

Lucille and Virginia loved the friendship between their husbands for two completely different reasons. Lucille enjoyed the simple fact that her husband had someone who acted as a surrogate brother to Eddie. He was an only child and never enjoyed the benefits of having the fights, debates, and jokes that brothers share. It was nice to see her husband get this opportunity. Virginia enjoyed hearing her husband let loose and laugh from time to time. Hearing John Sr. just relax and laugh made her relax. He was always so stoic and sincere that when she caught a glimpse of him leaning in to hear one of Eddie's dirty jokes and then bend in two to try to contain his eruption of laughter, she smiled from the inside out. She could not stop her entire face from smiling. She was grateful that John Sr. had Eddie. It was nice to see her husband have this.

Ponce's Deli was not only renowned for Eddie's jokes and the homemade delicacies of Lucille. To Michael and Sean Cloughey, it was an absolute wonderland filled with candy, ice cream, and comic books. However, nothing, absolutely nothing, could compare to a small section of the store that contained baseball cards. The Cloughey brothers agreed on very little throughout their lives, but when it came to baseball cards, they both found their true church in the statistics and individualized histories of the players on the cards themselves. It provided them with hours of shared time, and much of that time was spent conducting sophisticated debates, acts of appreciation, trade, diplomacy, and negotiation. They were the politicians of Ponce's Deli, and they could be heard, from time to time, laughing around the sealed packages of new cards and pondering which of Eddie's collectible cards they would buy that particular day. John Sr. never actually shared with anyone just how much he appreciated witnessing his boys enjoying being together. He could never tell his wife how much it wounded him to see his sons fight. He wanted to grab them both and sit them down and have that fatherly conversation about how they should get along, protect each other, and be there for one another. He knew that they were all they would have, and he knew that they could never understand how much they would absolutely hate themselves if they just dismissed each other and simply forgot one another. He would sit alone at the kitchen table some nights with his heavy, tired head in his wrinkled hands, internally practicing what he might say and how he might present the idea to them both.

Inevitably, he felt and understood that he just couldn't do it. They were just too different in nature to explain anything to. What was effective on Sean would prove a failure to Michael, and Michael just didn't have the patience that Sean had. He had seen Michael come home late at times in conditions that would make him shudder. He felt there was something wrong with his younger son. He saw the bruised knuckles, the split lips, the scraped cheekbones. John Sr. knew that he would only be able to keep Michael out of jail or out of a morgue for so long. He just wanted to beg Michael to wait until after he and his wife had passed away for Michael to commit some act that would get him arrested. John Sr. would lie to himself and say that he knew his wife would never be able to handle something like that happening to one of her sons when in truth he was the one it would destroy beyond consideration. He was, however, paralyzed to confront him about it. He knew he could appeal to Sean's reason and rationality regarding matters of life and maturity. Michael was a different breed, and his entire body had always carried itself in that way. So when the occasion presented itself and he could stop and just hear his sons sharing a joke or indulging in some conjoined happiness, he reveled in it. He wished it would be like that for their entire lives. He knew it wouldn't.

By their midteens, the Cloughey brothers, with the help of Edelberto Pena, had amassed an absolutely incredible collection of baseball cards. This collection was kept in pristine condition, and it was practically guarded over like the famous jewels of the Romanov family. Michael loved to collect the sluggers while Sean enjoyed the finesse players. Michael loved to trade, and Sean loved to preserve his stock. Michael loved to chew the thin piece of rectangular gum that came in many newly opened packages while Sean hated the gum but adored the smell and the sugary dust that the gum left behind on the cards. Baseball cards became the periodic peace accord that very briefly extended its olive branch between the Cloughey boys. Virginia loved the cease-fires, but John Sr. knew in his chest, right where the bottom of his heart met his stomach, that all wars get worse after peace treaties are broken.

———

IT WAS APPROXIMATELY 6:22 ON A SUNDAY MORNING when Edelberto Pena was awakened by his youngest son, Guillermo, who would work the store most weekend mornings. This would allow his mother to attend mass and allow his father to have just one day to sleep a little late.

"Papi, Michael is downstairs in the store."

"*Felicidades*, Mo. *Yo estoy cansado, por favor.*"

"No, Pa. Something's wrong."

"*Que paso?*"

"*Yo no se.* He won't say anything to me at all."

"*Ay, Dios.*"

Berto threw on his robe, tied the waist, and placed his cold feet into his slippers. He smoothed what was left of the hair on his head and placed his thick-lensed glasses on his round face. Guillermo had grown up in the same neighborhood as Michael Cloughey, and they played baseball together as young boys. Only a year younger than Michael, he was readily aware of the Dave Mantinakis incident from a little over a year prior. Guillermo worshipped Michael for his ability but he, like many others, was very afraid of Michael. However, he had never seen him quite like this. This was not anger. It was not rage. It was something he could not identify.

By the time Berto reached Michael, he knew something irreversible had occurred. People did not look the way Michael did at that moment under typical circumstances. Michael looked ashen and sleep deprived, and he was disheveled. As Berto tried to get him to sit down, he could hear Michael mumbling something. Berto instructed his son to close and lock the door to the store and flip the sign so it read "Closed" from the outside. Berto shuffled as quickly as he could in his slippers behind the counter and found a clean rag. He took that rag and dunked it into the ice container until it was frigid and completely saturated. What bothered Berto the most was that Michael's eyes looked like they were about to shut tightly. They were black underneath and appeared to be drooping He feared drugs were to blame; he worried that he had been in a fight and perhaps gotten hit so hard that a concussion might have settled in, if not worse. He started to ask Michael some questions that even a child would know.

"How many fingers do I have up?"

An incoherent mumbling came in response.

"What's your name?" That question was met with more mumbling and a shaking of his head.

Berto grabbed Michael by both shoulders and forced him to look in his eyes.

"Miguelito, what is wrong with you?"

Michael pulled his way free, leapt toward the garbage pail, and began violently throwing up. Berto sat forcibly back in a folding chair, one slipper on, the other off somewhere at his side. He was sweating and felt a tightening in his gut. He used the sleeve of his robe to wipe his face. He was trying to get his bearings, having been just roused out of sleep by this event, this scene. He felt slightly dizzy and questioned if he was having a dream. He leaned over and placed his elbows on his knees, and he took several deep breaths to right his equilibrium. Guillermo was silent and scared.

Michael finished and sat with his back against the wall and his knees up toward his chest. He used the bottom of his T-shirt to wipe his mouth and face. He had an acidic taste in his mouth, and he was having a hard time catching his breath. He rested his head back and closed his eyes. Michael could feel his heart beating in his ears and neck. He had heavy collections of sweat under his arms and down his back. His arms and legs were of little use, and he knew if he tried to stand, he would come crashing down. He decided to sit exactly where he was and focus his eyes on the display case where Eddie stored some of his most coveted baseball cards. He and Sean had spent hours hovering over this cabinet with anticipation and joy running through their entire body. This cabinet offered absolutely no relief at this moment, and Michael wondered if it ever would again. His stomach still felt as though it had more to divest itself of into Eddie's garbage pail. He felt the eyes of Eddie and Guillermo on him, waiting for a reveal. Michael said nothing.

There was a light knocking on the door and a muffled voice that said the name Eddie as if it were a question. Guillermo rushed to the front door of the store and unlocked it to find John Sr. standing in an outfit that could be best described as having been assembled spontaneously in the dark. John Sr. had a look on his face that Eddie had only seen a few times in his life. It was a combination of fear, confusion, and whatever one feels after they have surpassed exhaustion. Eddie placed his head in both of his hands, which were now shaking.

"*Madre de Dios.*"

Guillermo Pena stood off in the corner between the wall and the door opening, and he studied the room around him and the three individuals before him. He knew, by his father's exasperation, exactly what had happened and why all three of them looked the way they did. He looked at Michael and then the ground, and he felt his jaw tighten slightly. He wanted to be strong for his father, for his friend, and for John Sr., but he accepted his age, his inexperience, and his place in this room, and he began to cry deeply.

John Sr. saw his youngest son on the floor up against the wall, and he walked to him. When he got to Michael's feet, he squatted in front of him. He put both of his hands on Michael's knees. He knew at this moment that his son needed to feel warmth, love. His action also disguised the fact that he was about to collapse before his child.

"Michael, we have to go home."

"Why?"

"Because we're needed."

"Nobody needs us anymore."

"Sean needs us."

"That's not my house anymore."

"What are you saying? It will always be your house. Don't you ever say that to me."

"Fuck that house."

Eddie got up and made a quick gesture to his son. Both quickly walked into the back room of the store, and as Eddie passed John Sr., he put his hand on his shoulder. John Sr. didn't know what to do in response to this gesture, but a large part of him was grateful for it.

"I need you to come home with me, Michael. Please."

Michael looked down and shook his head silently making a response of "no."

John Sr. took a deep breath and looked at his son and found the strength to stand up. Eddie emerged from the back room holding a cup of coffee. He handed the cup to John Sr. and walked him to the door.

"He can stay with us. Go."

John Sr. said nothing. Eddie closed the door behind him and locked it. He flipped the lock and pulled the shade down over the window on the door. Ponce's would not open today. Eddie called for Guillermo, who was hovering right around the corner of the back room.

"*Papito*, wake up your mother. Do it gently."

Eddie sat back on the folding chair and pulled it a little closer to Michael. It was silent except for some light traffic outside. The early risers entering the world. There were still some sleeping, still some safe and secure in their beds. There were probably a few just getting home at this hour after a Saturday night filled with fun and laughter.

"Michael, there are three things I love more than anything in this world. I love my family, I love my beautiful island of Puerto Rico, and I love the game of baseball. Do you know why I love them?"

Michael put both of his hands over his face and exhaled deeply. He had no intention of answering any questions. He had no intention of trying to figure anything out. He didn't even have the intention of getting up off the floor.

"I love them so much because they require nothing of me in return except to love them back. They accept me and love me unconditionally. I appreciate them and respect them for what they are at all times. I never have to worry about impressing them or being something or someone else for them. They love me with the same passion whether I am at my highest or lowest point. They are good to me, and they fill me with love and joy and pride. But mostly I love them because they can never be taken away from me. No matter what happens in life I will always have them and they me. In my life I have experienced a rich collection of emotion. I have been wealthy when it comes to feeling. The easiest emotion to feel is love. It requires absolutely no work on the part of the person giving it. My family, my country, and my sport are so easy to love."

Michael parted the hands in front of his face and looked at the man sitting in front of him wearing an old robe and torn house slippers. Eddie's heavy eyes were staring off in a different direction, and his hands were loosely clasped together between his knees. Michael felt as though he were talking to himself just as much as him.

"*Miguelito*, your mother loved you very much. No matter where you are or where you will be, she will always love you. You will always have that. Always."

Virginia Cloughey had defeated the cancer that attacked her body, ravaged it, and drastically weakened it. She was not able, however, to defeat the massive heart attack that had occurred while she was sleeping during the early morning hours of August 17th.

Michael Cloughey looked at the black-rimmed clock over the doorway. It was 6:57 a.m.

The sun was coming up.

CHAPTER 21

ROBERT HANOVER SAT IN HIS CAR WITH THE EN-gine running and the windows rolled up, looking out of the driver's side window with an anticipation that he last felt when he was a small boy playing hide-and-seek. His older sister used to insist he hide first and then would begin counting loudly. Her voice would then trail off, and he would start to get that excited nervousness that would build throughout his entire body. She would then play that predictable game of yelling out, "I wonder if he is in here! Or here?" The tension would build, and his heart would start beating faster. A minute or so later, she would quickly open the closet door or lift the sheet on the bed to find him curled up in a ball. He would scream and she would laugh, and they would both fall to the floor laughing only to recreate the entire act all over again.

This game was different, however. Hanover needed to be seen, and he needed Nia Antoine to get him her brother's phone.

There had to be something on this phone that was the cause of this bullshit. He had limited time to put this fire out, and the longer she kept him waiting the harder it would be. Sitting in this neighborhood, in this car, at this time, was not his idea of a good time. He had already put Anya on doing some research on the teacher, but he felt that this phone was the shortcut and the real answer as to why a teacher would throw his entire life away. He was growing impatient with the situation, growing irritated with DiNardi, and growing extremely angry with the thought that this fucking teacher could destroy something he had no idea about. His eyes felt heavy, and his body needed to be horizontal. He closed his eyes for just a moment and pinched the bridge of his nose with his thumb and forefinger. Just as he was able to finally allow himself a moment to relax, a rapid and loud rapping made him sit bolt upright in his seat. For a moment he forgot where the button was to lower his window. Nia had used her brother's phone to tap on the window, and she was now holding it up for him to see as if it were some prize she had won. She had a huge smile on her face, and Hanover could have sworn she was doing a little dance.

"Where is your brother?"

"They gave him some pain medicine at the hospital, so when he fell asleep, I went through this stuff and found it. I don't know the code to his phone, though. Is that okay?"

"That is the best news I have received all day. Don't worry about the code. I have someone who can handle all of that."

Hanover took the phone and placed it in the inside pocket of his jacket, and from the same pocket, he withdrew a beige business envelope. He handed one end to Nia Antoine, and when she went to grab the other end from him, he squeezed his end so she could not take it. She looked at him, puzzled.

"This is what we spoke about on the phone earlier. Listen to me very carefully because I will not repeat myself and I mean everything I am about to say."

Nia's body tightened. This did not look like the Robert Hanover from earlier in the day, and his voice did not possess the sweet disposition from earlier on the phone. She kept a grip on the envelope, not because of its contents but because she was afraid of what might happen to her if she let go and ran.

"None of this happened. You were not contacted by me, we never spoke in any fashion, and we never met. You never gave me this phone, and you have no idea what happened at school today. As a matter of fact, you don't even know what I look like and you will never speak my name out loud except for when I end this conversation and you respond, 'Yes, Mr. Hanover.' If anything should happen to violate any of this agreement and I find out that it is your doing, you will be paid a visit by someone who is not me. This person will not possess the tact and polish that I do. I promise you that this person will be very fond of underage girls, especially underage girls who are virgins."

Hanover ended his last sentence with a half smile that only affected his mouth. His eyes retained their intensity, and at that moment, his eyes were locked on the eyes of Nia Antoine. She felt a fear she had never felt before.

"Do you understand me?"

"Yes, Mr. Hanover."

"Excellent. Have fun at Yale."

Hanover closed his window and adjusted himself in his seat. He shifted into drive and quickly put a city block distance between Nia and himself. He carefully checked his mirrors and called Anya.

"Are you on your way back to the office?"

"Yes. I completed my errand successfully."

"I don't know why you didn't let me get it."

"Quite all right. I find the young Ms. Antoine bright and rather charming. I offered her your job upon the completion of her studies at Yale. She said yes."

"Fuck you, Mr. Hanover. Pick me up a coffee on your way here."

"I don't have time to stop for that, Anya."

"Fuck you twice. Yes, you do, or you can spend the entire night trying to break the passcode to the kid's phone yourself."

Robert could tell that first "Fuck you" was Anya's sarcasm. He was certain the second one was draped in sincerity. He worded his next question professionally.

"Did you have time to make that other call I asked you so kindly to make?"

"Yes, Mr. Hanover, I most certainly did."

"Thank you, Anya. See you in a few."

By the time Robert Hanover had completed his phone call with Anya, Nia Antoine was sitting on her bed behind the locked door of her bedroom. The envelope she had just received was placed in the third drawer of her dresser beneath two winter sweaters and one green wool scarf. She hated the two sweaters because they made her itchy, and the scarf had been knitted for her by her grandmother as a gift for Nia's sixteenth birthday last year. Sitting on her bed, she was most certain that she had just made an enormous mistake. She was not sure who the mistake would eventually affect, but she was most certain that it was much larger than what was in that envelope she had just hidden beneath the two sweaters and the scarf.

CHAPTER 22

Sean pulled up a block away from Ponce's Deli and put his car in park. He left his right hand on the gearshift and his left hand on the wheel. Sean was reluctant to remove his hands from the position they currently occupied. If he removed the keys, it would lead to him turning the car off. If he turned the car off, it would lead to him getting out of the car. If he got out of the car, it would lead to him walking down the block and seeing his brother, and this would lead to him having to hear the story behind yet another delightful chapter of gothic literature created by Michael Cloughey.

They had not seen each other nor spoken to one another in a very long time. Sean did not know it was possible to feel such a large range of emotions and yet seemingly feel nothing at all. There were many times that Sean felt the need, the want, and the obligation to call Michael. Although there was no formal request or invitation, he was certain that his mother would have wanted him to be the more responsible one. Their father, if he were not caught in the throes of Alzheimer's disease, would have appreciated and perhaps even expected Sean to be the stronger of his two sons. It was thoughts like this that drove Father Sean Cloughey to sleepless nights. A part of him wanted to be the classic big brother who put his arm around his younger sibling and then proceed to solve all his problems. He wanted to be a brother-in-law to Lara, and he wanted to be a proud uncle who would gladly spoil his nephew. Would a part of this be compensation for never having a son of his own? Was a part of this jealousy that he held somewhere? Perhaps he was jealous of the life that Michael led? Perhaps he wanted to have the internalized freedom to destroy anyone he disliked or disagreed with. It must be so very freeing to be able to crack open the skin of someone you felt deserved it, to make them bleed, to make them feel agony, to make them feel shame for not being able to defeat you. To never possess the fear of being hit in the face or shiver at the thought of being hit in the stomach so square and hard that it loosened your bowels was the very recipe that constructed his brother.

The other side of Sean's brain told him that his brother was a prick who deserved every fucking hardship he ever faced in life. Michael had been getting away with everything short of murder since he was born. He treated people like shit. He kicked the shit out of people without so much as a "Oh, I'm sorry I beat your face in." He had sex with any girl that had a pulse and a working mouth, and to make worse what was already a car crash combined with a horror movie, he did all of this with an unblemished sense of righteousness. It was as if he were placed here to pull the nails from the palms of Christ and to beat the shit out of every Roman soldier who had hammered one of those nails into place. Who the fuck did he think he was anyhow?

It was their parents who had created Michael. They were the ones who constantly pulled him out of trouble like a baby out of a burning orphanage. They coddled and supported the torture and brutality that Michael dispensed for much of his life. Their mother saw a goodness somewhere deep inside of Michael that Sean just did not see. He would have given quite a bit in exchange for even a glimpse of what Virginia Cloughey had seen in her youngest son. But then again, Sean, unlike his mother, had been victimized by Michael. Much of Sean's decisions regarding his brother, as well as his actions around his brother, all evolved to some degree out of fear. Sean was afraid of Michael, and even though his faith and his teachings told him otherwise, he did not want to give Michael any more opportunities to hurt or even destroy him, or anyone else for that matter. Sean felt certain that he could, if necessary, hold his own against his brother, but was this really the way to expend your thoughts when it came to your family, your sibling—feeling pretty sure that you could fend off a person of extreme physical violence? The fork to the face episode that he and Michael had shared many years ago could be perceived of as a pure stroke of luck on Sean's part in taking Michael by surprise, or, for the more confident in the room, it could be viewed as meeting toe-to-toe and besting his brother.

The truth was that Sean had waited most of his adult life for a call much like the one he had recently received from Michael. However, most of his nightmares circulated around a cop telling him that Michael was in prison for killing someone or that Michael had been killed by someone capable of more violence than he was. It was this very reason that Sean just felt unable to engage with Michael. There were so many days that Sean's hand was on the phone or he had just finished watching a movie and wanted to share it with someone. There were even times that Sean saw a play during a game that would make him believe in the purity of baseball, and he would have this urge to say "Fuck it" and call his brother. Lately, he had been fighting the urge to just call Sean and ask about his son. He knew very well how his nephew was doing because he spoke to Lara quite frequently without Michael finding out. He had begged Lara not to tell Michael of his calls and his concern. He had made her promise not to let Michael know he had sent birthday gifts and cards to his nephew. There was even one day when Lara had felt insistent that he just sit down with Michael to talk that he reminded her that he was a priest and that she could not reverse her promise. They shared a laugh that was reserved for friends with an inside joke or for family that was family. It was nice to have a sister. It was nice to have someone to talk to and laugh with. It was nice to share in a warm and sincere way.

Sean never felt the existence of that with his brother, and even if he did, just how do you allow yourself to get close to someone that you are most certain will end up paying for their sins in the most complicated of ways? How do you pal around with someone you are positive allows a certain amount of violence to take up residency inside them? Evil is one thing when you allow it to pay rent and stay for some distinct amount of time. However, when one allows an evil to just move in free of charge, eat their groceries, and put its feet up on their coffee table, that is quite a different tale of woe. Sean prayed that his brother would walk into his confessional and admit to and apologize for all the things he had done. That action would be a bookmark, a starting point, a road flare. *"Dear God, it has been six months since my last confession. I hit one of my students because they didn't pass their midterm exam."*

All these things occupied space in the mind and soul of Sean Cloughey. These things clawed at various points of him at various times. They challenged him and made him hate, pity, and suffer wild pangs of confusion over his brother. So when the phone rang today and Sean heard Michael's voice, he did not quite know the emotion to attach to it at all. Michael's inflection sounded off and his usual matter-of-fact expression was absent. He sounded wounded. He sounded resigned. Sean's instinct was to hang up, but when he heard the tone in Michael's voice and then the explanation, a part of his more magnanimous side wanted to scream, "You see, you stupid ass, I told you!"

There was another part of him that felt a joyous relief. It was a feeling that Sean could only compare to the doctor telling you that your blood tests came back and it is nothing after all. Then the guilt settled in, and all the blood rushed to Sean's head when Michael told him what he had done. It is very much a vomit-inducing moment when someone tells you what you have feared would come true. It is a moment when you wonder just how much of yourself can take it and how much of yourself would be able to move past it. He was not quite sure how he hung up the phone and got to his car, he really had no clue how he was able to drive, and he was not quite sure how his brother would look or what he would say in return. All Sean Cloughey knew was that he was about to get out of his car and see his brother for the first time in years and get introduced to yet another grisly episode of violence in the life of Michael Cloughey.

Sean looked at himself in the rearview mirror, and he adjusted his collar. On days he was not scheduled to perform an anointing or serve over a funeral, Sean would dress in a rather relaxed manner. Today, his frame was covered in a pair of jeans with a button-down blue Oxford shirt and a broken-in pair of brown loafers. Although the exterior looked comfortable and relaxed, his insides felt twisted, contorted. Today, he felt his age.

He got out of his car and immediately smelled ozone in the air. He knew that a thunderstorm was on its way. Sean always loved the rain—the smell of it, the feel of it. Most people associated the rain with an ominous foreboding. Sean admired how the rain could speed everything up while simultaneously slowing things down. It forced people to run for shelter, and it made those inside thankful to be somewhere dry. It wasn't like snow that left a coating for days at a time. During the warmer months, the rain would come down and make its presence felt and just as quickly vanish, leaving behind a hot, steaming pavement that would eventually show no traces of it.

Sean disliked the fact that this family reunion of sorts was taking place on a day when he could sense the oncoming storm and not find himself in a chair reading a book. He also disliked the fact that Michael chose Ponce's Deli for their "greeting card" moment. Mr. Pena, at his age, did not need to bear witness to whatever nonsense was about to be thrown around his store. The Pena family had spent more than enough time dealing with Cloughey family bullshit. They had been more than generous in the wake of their mother's death and their father losing almost every inch of his former self to Alzheimer's. Mr. Pena, now in his late eighties, had lost his wife five years ago. Guillermo had pretty much taken over the store from his father, who was still mourning the death of his wife and the hospitalization of his good friend, John Sr. Sean had not been inside Ponce's for many years, but as he now grabbed the door handle, he felt the presence of the little boy who had eventually picked his brother up off the floor to carry him home the evening after their mother had died.

The bell over the door signaling the entrance of a customer was still the same, but the inside had been given a completely updated and modernized look. It was obvious that Guillermo was serious about taking the store into the next generation of Penas, but he hadn't forgotten to retain some of the old-fashioned touches that people in the neighborhood found nostalgic. The tin ceilings were restored, and the wood trim around the doorways and moldings had been stripped down to their natural wood and refinished with a dark stain. The tables had been fixed, and the metal stools at the lunch counter were re-upholstered. So as not to lose the authenticity of the old-fashioned diner/deli appearance, all the signs and advertising had been restored with neon and the appropriate framing. Sean smirked at the restoration of the flooring tile, which had been brought back to capture the true charm of the black-and-white checkerboard pattern. The neighborhood kids used to play a game where they would have to enter the store to make their purchase without stepping on a specific color, one day white and the other day black. Had Sean been entering Ponce's Deli for the first time, he would have thought he had been propelled neatly into the past; he also would have asked for a job stocking the shelves or working the old-fashioned nickel-plated National Cash Register. More modern deli and grocery stores were all converting to computerized inventory with Q coding and UPC scanners, many of which even allowed customers to check themselves out with no human interaction whatsoever. The National Cash Register made a sound distinctive with a specific time in history, much like the old-fashioned Royal or Remington typewriters of their day. There are some sounds and smells that take you to a place that you might have been at one time. They also made many wish that they had never left or became scarce or extinct.

Guillermo, working the National, was the first person Sean made eye contact with when he entered the store. The beauty of the store and seeing Mo for the first time in years was almost enough to make Sean forget why he was here. The inevitable meeting he was about to experience was not something he was looking forward to. He was expecting that it would only dampen the impression and the nostalgia of the new Ponce's Deli. Mo, at the moment, could only exchange two gestures; the first was a smile with a combined raise of both eyebrows that displayed his happiness at seeing an old friend, and the second was a head motion that was a well-executed combination between a nod and a wave. The second gesture did not require the services of an interpreter; Michael was in the back room.

CHAPTER 23

ROBERT HANOVER WALKED PAST ANYA'S DESK AND placed Stanley Antoine's phone on her full-size desk calendar. As he started to remove his jacket, he simultaneously handed her the coffee she ordered. Hanover could be extremely deft and economical with words and movements when the matter at hand called for it. Grabbing the door handle to his office, he looked at his watch and said, "Dance." This was both a word that at times evoked encouragement and at others was meant to light a fire under Anya. Robert knew that Anya's productivity level was much higher than most individuals. He also knew that, while she was confident, Anya loved the recognition that her talents were exceptional. She was also the one person who enjoyed a challenge almost as much as her boss. When Robert used this term, he was encouraging her to do what her talents afforded as well as get it done as quickly as humanly possible. It was no matter what their unique coding afforded them in terms of interpretation or true understanding; Anya was very much aware that this specific job was one of the most significant she had ever been given, and in this instance, their terminology was entirely unnecessary. She looked at the cell phone and then referred to her Matson rose ormolu desk clock. The clock was a gift from her grandmother, whose nickname for Anya was "Rose." Every time Anya looked at the beautiful detail that its maker put into the rose on the very top of the clock, she thought of her grandmother. It always made her smile no matter how pressed for time she was.

Now that Robert was safely tucked in his office and could offer no distractions, she got to work. She took a sip of her coffee and took a deep breath to get the red blood cells moving. She would need to get through the password on this phone and find the true cause of their problem. Forecasting this as a singular challenge was a growth mindset she had developed for herself. She was both excited by the challenge and somewhat nervous. If she fucked this up, she was almost certain that there would be a few people either leaving the country or taking a few matters into their own hands. A job like this could take hours that they simply did not have. She adored the challenge.

Twelve minutes and thirty-seven seconds later, Anya placed both of her hands at the edge of her desk and pushed her chair away. Stanley Antoine's phone was propped up against the corner of her monitor. She stared intently at her computer with a look that combined feelings of curiosity, satisfaction, and absolute confusion. Anya was unsure as to which of those feelings she should take ownership of, but she picked up her desk phone anyway.

"Robert."

"Shouldn't you be working, Anya?"

"Two things: I'm done, and we have a problem."

CHAPTER 24

Sᴇᴀɴ Cʟᴏᴜɢʜᴇʏ ᴏᴘᴇɴᴇᴅ ᴀɴᴅ ᴡᴀʟᴋᴇᴅ ᴛʜʀᴏᴜɢʜ ᴀ wooden door that was one of the original leftovers from the old Ponce's. The door had the original brass kickplate at the bottom as well as the original brass lock set with skeleton key fixture. Both items contained just the right amount of patina to suggest years of existence as well as the charm that life contained. While others would have sold the brass for a few dollars, Mo retained their services, and they added another small bit of character to his shop. The doorknob itself was a round ivory ball. Doorknobs and lock sets at that time were usually an all-brass construction with either ivory or glass doorknobs. Skeleton keys eventually gave way to the pin tumbler system and heavy cast aluminum in the 1940s, but they and their brass lock set relative represented something—craftsmanship. Things used to be made to last: wooden doors, brass lock sets, tin ceilings, even old cash registers. If something lasted, it was symbol of pride. If something lasted, it meant that it was meant to be and have purpose. If something lasted, it meant that it would be around for a while, and that you could appreciate it for just being. However, things were not made to last anymore. Things were now meant to be used up and disposed of. Things were meant to become outdated and insignificant rather quickly. The faster you could purchase the next item in the series, the better. Who did this? Who made things to just discard? What was the purpose of having anything if the next was better? Who determined that the next was better, more significant, more advanced?

Father Cloughey spoke of these things during Sunday services with frequency. He spoke of people and their lack of patience, understanding, and lack of appreciation for what was around them and what they had. He warned of the dangers of excessive want, avarice, and how it made the heart ugly and how it clouded the mind and most importantly, the soul. One time at a Bible group, he became engaged in a lengthy and impassioned conversation with a young man who argued that it was our place to keep advancing and pressing forward to find the next best thing, the ultimate of everything. He offered that it was our God-given right and our obligation to keep improving all and everything: "If God did not want us to continue striving, he would not have provided us with the intellect to make advancements in the fields of science, art, and technology."

Father Cloughey lightly nodded in agreement and looked into eyes of the young man and then turned his head to the left and right to look at the other parishioners sitting around him. He removed his forefinger from the book of Psalms and replaced it with a thin silk ribbon that was dark blue. It had been extracted from the Book of Matthew where two of his favorite passages resided. He put his Bible face down on the table in front of him, placed his flattened right hand down, and on top of that, he placed his flattened left hand. He leaned forward slightly so that his chest leaned against the table in front of him.

"I agree with so much of what you are saying, and I believe fully that we should not waste the talents and abilities that God granted us with. To do that would be shameful, a travesty, and it goes without saying that it would be considered by some to be a sin. However, at what cost do we sacrifice and potentially give up on things so easily? When we consistently practice the art of disposal in our lives of work and business, do we not think that it carries into our everyday social life? This is more than just upgrading a cell phone or consistently updating a social media page. How quickly do people give up on their marriage and reach out to another? How often do we quit jobs or give up on a task when it becomes too complicated? How often do we give up on someone we care about because it is just easier to avoid them or not have to put up with habits that may put us out?"

"But Father, don't you feel that we have made huge strides in life itself and in what we as people are capable of doing? Surgeries, robotics, curing disease…How are these things—"

"Donald, I am not saying that we should not strive to be better. I am saying that when we consistently practice removing things from our lives because they are last year's model or the old operating system, we lose track of what is truly important to keep and hold on to. How much of it is done out of competition? How much is truly jealousy? How much is just having the money to do it and show it off? Why do people really wait on a line for days to get a new phone when they have a similar version only twelve months older in their pocket, knowing full well that it will be available without waiting only a few days later?"

"Isn't that their right, Father? Isn't that their practice of a true and proper experience in free will? That they have the freedom to buy it? They have the right to stand in line if they wish, and they have the right to spend the money they earned on whatever they want to stand in line for?"

"They do have the right and the choice and the free will to do all of that. We were given an intellect to make decisions and to choose, but I speak of the morality of the thing itself. The ethical quandary that technologically offers up is that for all the advancements that technology has made, it has *not* made us better people. Technology has not made us more morally and spiritually sound. It has made us the opposite of moral and ethical. In what ways are we kinder, more compassionate, more loving? - Forget the Bible and its teachings."

Sean pushed the Bible in front of him to the edge of the table and put his hands up in a "surrender position. He sat back and with an open left hand he swept it around the room at those around him as if they could deposit an answer into his palm. Some were captivated by this debate while others displayed a discomfort expressed in their shifting in their chairs. One older woman wrinkled her brow and pushed her head back in disbelief when Sean mentioned forgetting the Bible entirely.

"Yes, this is what I am saying. Let us simply forget that we have religion for a moment and forget that we have a dogma that guides it and its practices. Let us say that we are simply governed by the free will you discussed earlier. Why has that free will and all the offerings of modern technology made us blindly bully the weak online and subject others to ridicule and wrestle the virtue out of the most innocent individuals, but that same free will has not allowed us to act more altruistically? That cell phone in your possession allows you to call and connect with anyone in this world in several different ways, yet we use it to disconnect from each other just as equally. And with that we forfeit our morality and our virtue. When we can replace so much of what is around us, we hold nothing, including life, in esteem."

"Are you blaming poverty and genocide and harassment on my cell phone, Father?"

The room laughed lightly because Father Cloughey smiled at the question and put his head in his hands. He looked around the room again and found that his eyes were met with the smiles and generous head nodding and light applause of those who had just been exposed to a satisfying seminar in theology, philosophy, and sociology. He applauded back and spoke over the clapping. "I believe this is a good place to stop for the night." He picked up his Bible and held it up for the room to see. He held it over his head and waved it slightly. "Please pay attention to the Book of James for next week, and if anyone would like to have their voice heard, I am sure that Donald and I would be more than happy to relinquish the pulpit for a little while."

Later that evening, Sean had a chance to do what most people do. He relived some of the events of his day and recalled the conversation with Donald. He was happy that the discussion had happened, and he felt proud that he had the opportunity to share an important stance on morality. It was nice to have a spirited debate with someone who could hold their own while upholding the appropriate standards of such debate. His mind brought him to his points on relationships, and he could not help but feel like a well-practiced hypocrite. He knew he had given up on Michael. Sean was torn, and he felt somewhat immobilized by the feelings that came with the experience. He had known for some time that he should have made amends with his brother and tried everything he possibly could to at least resolve some of the issues that stood between them. But, as Lara had mentioned once, their issues were oceans, and their problems were mountains.

It was that debate with Donald Tressell, a twenty-six-year-old financial estate planner at a highly reputable financial institution, in the parish conference room on a late Wednesday afternoon that brought Father Sean Cloughey to Ponce's and to the doorknob that he had just released. As Sean fully entered the room, which had been converted to an actual working office from a large, dusty storage closet, he scanned the room to find it empty.

"Michael?"

There was no response in return. Sean opened the door to the bathroom and turned on the light. There was still no sign of his brother. He looked under Mo's desk and behind the couch, and he finally opened a large, heavy metal door on the opposite side of the room. It led to a small open space, and the more he pushed the door open, the more light entered the room behind him. Sean stepped outside into a tiny courtyard that could only be entered by the door he was about to close. Across from him, approximately twelve to fifteen feet away, was the back of the opposing building, and to his left and right were two walls capped by barbed wire. Michael sat on a blue plastic milk crate with the words "Ruddin Farms" imprinted in white on the side. Michael quickly picked his head up to spot his brother, and he then put his face down into both of his open hands.

"Michael."

There was no verbal response, but one of Michael's legs began to anxiously bounce up and down. His clothes were a conglomeration of wrinkles, sweat, and dirt, and the backs of his hands still retained the scars of his past. Michael's left middle knuckle also displayed what appeared to be a fresh bone bruise and reddish abrasion.

"Michael, what is going on? Are you ok? Why are you here?"

Sean slid a wooden shipping palette over to the right of the milk crate and placed a plastic bucket down on top of it. He dusted off the bottom of the bucket before sitting. This construct put Sean at a higher eye level than Michael. He knew this would be the case when he decided to build his seat. He did not know what method of greeting to use at this moment. He was confused about so many things, and there were so many things between them that had not been addressed, properly worked through, or even forgotten. All Sean understood was that if anything productive was to come of this family reunion on plastic, it would have to be from his initiation and prodding.

He had been here for only a few minutes, and he already felt fatigued. Michael had a way of invisibly exhausting those around him. It was not so much the fact that he was difficult to deal with, although that was a possibility; it was more what he was capable of. The potential energy that he owned and that he operated all his functions with was leechlike in its existence. How was Lara able to live a moderately successful life filled with loving experiences in which she was able to express what appeared to be sincere happiness while married to his brother?

What was exactly admirable or suitable about Michael as a partner? These questions floated through Sean's head for years, and they often found themselves resting right behind his eyes above his nose. They usually led to a headache that would reside in his face for hours. Father Cloughey had begged, prayed, and pleaded with God to the point of making ridiculous deals that he knew no normal human being would ever be able to uphold if God would just be able to provide him with an answer to what made his brother lovable. One night following a midnight mass Christmas service, he promised God that he would spend the remainder of his life doing missionary work if God would just provide him with some glimpse as to a lovable quality that resided in his brother. Needless to say, Father Cloughey never found himself booking any flights to countries in need of convergence and spiritual awakening. While he was moderately thankful that he was allowed the ability to remain in his parish, he became increasingly frustrated by the fact that perhaps no answer to this question would be found. As with so many frustrating life experiences, this led to resentment, which led to anger, and while he tried to control it and keep those existing thoughts at bay, he was at this moment enraged by the person sitting in front of him.

Why couldn't this phone call have occurred years before, months before, days before the event that caused it? Why hadn't Michael just called him one day to say, "Hey, Sean, it's Michael. Yeah, I know I'm a dick and I fucked up, and I said shit I shouldn't have and done things I shouldn't have and punched people who didn't deserve it and fucked women who should have been fucked by a better guy and in general just treated everyone like dog shit, but I think it's time we sat down and at least figured out how to treat each other like human beings."

But that call never came—ever. What Sean Cloughey did get was a short, panicked phone call that sounded dire in delivery, which led him to get in his car and drive to a childhood gathering place filled with varying memories, one regarding his mother that he would rather have forgotten forever, to a front row bucket seat to experience a badger having an angry and anxiety-filled life crisis.

What do we do when we are met with a formidable and immovable object or force? Sean Cloughey thought this to himself as he pushed his bucket closer to his brother and put his left arm around his brother's shoulder.

CHAPTER 25

MICHAEL SLID HIS HANDS DOWN HIS FACE, KEEPING his elbows on his knees. He picked his head up very slightly and inhaled deeply as his hands formed a supportive structure between his knees. He felt sweat running down his chest and stomach under his dress shirt, and he could smell the salty sweat that had gathered, lingered, and soaked into his hair and temples and face. He just wanted to sleep but knew he would never be able to sleep again the way he had just the night prior. Michael never truly slept peacefully. He had always been prone to bad dreams, night terrors, and late-night panic attacks that caused him crippling anxiety. He usually found himself feeling as though he was about to die—truly die—and his heart would beat faster, he would feel a numbness in his fingers and toes, and his entire body would get increasingly hot up through his head. This physical feeling would lead to nervousness, and then lead him to tell himself that it would be okay. This never worked, and that lack of success led to him get nauseous and sleepy and dizzy and his blood pressure would drop. His eyes would feel like anvils, so he would give up trying to keep them open. The only thing that would help relieve this panic would be movement, and he would get up and force himself to walk. It simply did not matter where he walked, who he walked with, or what time it was—he had to move. He attempted to walk until he either collapsed from exhaustion or until his muscles lost all ability to expand and contract. Today he could have walked to Jupiter, and there would be no relieving the amount of anxiety he felt at this moment.

"Sean, do you remember Christopher Murthaw?"

Sean immediately sat upright and snapped his head in the direction of his brother. Aside from the brief phone call he received summoning him to the bucket he was currently sitting on, he had not heard his brother's voice in person in a very long time. He was not sure if it was Michael's present state, but he just didn't remember his brother's voice having this much gravel in it. It sounded weaker, like thunder in the distance. Sean was also somewhat surprised that this question was Michael's lead statement given the current circumstances they both found themselves in. Lastly, Sean had no idea who Christopher Murthaw was, but he was highly curious how Mr. Murthaw played into this episode of the Cloughey brothers sitcom that was currently airing. Sean sighed in a volume loud enough so it could be interpreted as a loss of patience.

"No, I don't, Michael."

"Chris Murthaw, the guy who used to coach the boys' youth basketball team for the church? He was about a year or two older than you?"

"I have no idea who you are talking about here. Is he why I am here at this moment?"

"Maybe…"

"Maybe? Michael, what the—"

"All right, stop."

"Stop? Stop what? We haven't spoken in I don't know how long after what was just the most greeting card conversation two brothers could have. You call me earlier sounding like a mortician, and now I'm here and you want to play guessing games? Did you bring cards? I would have brought a board game if I knew we were going to have family fun time."

"This was a mistake."

"What's a mistake, Michael? You calling me here? Us as brothers? What exactly?"

"I hit one of my students today."

Sean winced and felt lightheaded. He had witnessed and experienced firsthand what Michael's hands felt like when they were used in that way. He thought about this kid, the student, wondering if the kid was in the hospital. He closed his eyes, took a breath, and exhaled through his nose. He was trying to compartmentalize the numerous questions that were attempting to escape from his mouth. He looked at Michael's hands—his knuckles to be precise—and saw what he thought was bruising; however, Michael's hands had taken on such a strange hue and form from the years of activity he put on them. When they were growing up, Sean would always catch sidelong glances at Michael's hands to see if there was any fresh activity. This observation of his brother, especially when he came in late or appeared annoyed, became somewhat of a habit. Honestly, it had been so long since Sean had seen his brother that he simply forgot to do it today, and he felt as though he let himself down for forgetting. Not having seen his brother or his knuckles in so long had thrown him off his usual prideful ability to predict people's current situation. The way in which people spoke, their breathing or lack thereof, their cadence, and overall carriage were telltale signs of their current situation. Sean felt something over the phone, but he honestly thought, based upon Michael's brief verbiage and the sudden contact out of nowhere, that perhaps even Michael could have downplayed the tragic nature of his actions. All Sean could manufacture at this moment was "How bad?"

"Bad…I think…I don't know, actually. It's not the first time." Michael offered up the last part of his fractured sentence seemingly as reconciliation. He added, "They made me leave. I don't really have any details. I—I think the kid went to the hospital."

"Wait, Michael. What do you mean it's not the first time? You have been hitting students? I don't…you have to start from the beginning here. I'm totally lost."

"Christopher Murthaw was a guy from the neighborhood who coached basketball and hung out with some of the same guys we know."

"Again with Christopher Murthaw? How does this—?"

Michael sat up straight and put his head back. His overall posture immediately became one of power, and his eyes became pin-focused on his brother. His eyebrows formed a point at their respective tops. He no longer needed his hands and elbows for support. "It does. It all does. It all connects. It always has, Sean. It all fucking connects to make me what I am. It is all about what I am right at this moment and what my entire life has been about up until this fucking backyard and this milk crate."

Sean didn't understand what his brother was saying, but he did understand when it was time to listen to someone else. He put both of his elbows on his knees and leaned forward toward Michael, bringing himself to Michael's eye level. "Okay, Mikey, who is Christopher Murthaw?"

CHAPTER 26

MICHAEL SAT FORWARD AND TOLD HIS BROTHER A story. He told Sean about Chris Murthaw. He told him that Chris was a kid a little older than them who traveled in the same neighborhood circles. He told Sean that he should remember Chris, but he could see how he might not. He told him that it wasn't even important if Sean remembered him or not.

The important part of the story was that several months after Dave Mantinakis, things were surprisingly and fairly calm in the life of Michael Cloughey. There were little to no incidents, no uprisings, no events, no coups d'état, no jihads, nothing of the sort. Michael had seemed to get it all out of his system that day in the visitors' dugout. He had escaped being arrested, going to jail, and perhaps experiencing a wealth of incarceration. He would have been free from retribution because the Mantinakis Incident put Michael on a veritable billboard of individuals you simply did not fuck with. Those who didn't know Michael from his baseball reputation knew Michael from the absolute destruction of Dave. It was so disturbing that Virginia and John Sr. even contemplated moving on two distinct occasions. When the talk of moving became loud enough for the house to hear, Michael played it cool and kept a lower profile than a hen in a fox house. Michael was very much aware that moving meant physically packing everything up and going to a city that they probably wouldn't be able to spot on a highly detailed map. This wasn't really the part of the orchestration that bothered Michael. He didn't have much to pack, and he didn't care much for what was around him. The part that would receive the asterisk, the exclamation point, in that debate and conversation, however, was that moving meant leaving everything here behind, including a one Miss Lara Trammell. That was something that Michael certainly did care about and certainly did not want to leave behind.

Michael went out very little, and when he did go out, it was usually with Lara and sometimes Sean. He also went to places where he knew people: the church teen center, Berto's store, the homes of his immediate friends. Sometimes he would just stay home. He would work out in the basement, read an insane amount of comic books, and spend an impossible amount of time playing dominoes with Yah.

John Sr. began to refer to Michael's habits as his son's new Spartan lifestyle. Michael enjoyed this ribbing because it came shortly after the two-week phase in which his father had threatened to enlist him in the military. Sean had to reassure Michael, in the few private conversations they had, that their father was only joking. However, Sean was not completely positive that a notion that drastic had not seriously crossed the mind of John Sr.

It was with all this information that Michael decided that existing, just existing, was his goal. It was a fairly young age to resign himself to this thought process, but he didn't have baseball anymore. He was regarded differently by those around him, and he had caused those closest to him an incredible amount of pain. Lastly, Michael understood something that his father had suspected, his mother denied, his brother was afraid of, and his girlfriend was trying to avoid for a very long time: there was something inside of him that just was not right. He just did not feel right. He felt it somewhere, but it had no identifying features or marks for him to take to a doctor and say, "Hey, doctor, see this mark? Well, what have you got to make it go away?" So the recognition of this thing and the ability to correct it were two things that resided in very different hemispheres.

One day when Michael was playing a game of pickup basketball in the church recreational center with a few friends and some guys that frequented the place on the weekends, his mind seemed to be in the right place, and, perhaps because of the exercise, he physically felt good. During one break toward the end of their game, one of the youth coaches asked Michael how much longer they would be. There was a scheduled practice for the youth parish team and approximately twelve ten-year-olds in mismatched uniforms were attempting to stretch and warm up. Michael took a second to recall the score and responded that they should be off in just a few minutes. Those "few minutes" turned into seventeen minutes, and a now impatient youth basketball coach passed on a sarcastic "farewell" with an additional murmur under his breath that only Michael was close enough to hear. Michael turned and apologized to the kids for taking as long as they had, and as they ran onto the court, he turned to their coach and said something that could not have been more than a few words. The coach responded with "You're an asshole. No one here is afraid of you" as Michael walked away. Michael had an enormous smile on his face. It was the one that showed a large portion of his teeth. It was the smile that Lara and many other young women absolutely adored. It was also the smile that Sean kept a rather distinct lookout for. It was his mother's smile.

At 8:17 p.m. the following Monday, Christopher Murthaw "walked" into the emergency room of Methodist Hospital. He was disheveled in appearance and his speech was slow and confused. He had bloodstains that ran down his right cheek, and his left pant leg was torn from mid-shin down to the ankle. He was missing one sneaker. He was quickly ushered past the registration area and onto a gurney in the hallway. A young female doctor and two nurses immediately checked him for stab wounds, gunshot wounds, and internal bleeding. As they were completing their initial examination, they bombarded him with a series of questions regarding his injuries. His right hand was visibly broken, and his right cheek had swollen up to the size of a golf ball. He had a deep gash on the inside of his lip that was the culprit for the tributary of blood on his shirt. Chris spent four days in the hospital and two months getting physical rehabilitation on his writing hand. He told the doctors in the ER, his family doctor, his rehabilitation therapist, his relatives, and his close friends that he had gotten his ankle stuck in the banister of the staircase in his home and he simply lost his footing and tumbled headfirst down the stairs. It was one of those things that could happen to anyone, and he was actually "pretty lucky" it wasn't worse. One of the receiving nurses in the emergency room remarked to a colleague that she didn't know that much about luck, but she sure as hell knew that it looked like he fell twenty flights of stairs.

CHAPTER 27

"JESUS CHRIST."

"I know, Sean."

Michael had spent the better part of an hour telling Sean what he was. He told him why he did what he did to Dave Mantinakis, Chris Murthaw, and several other individuals, and this portion of his admission included why he hit Stanley Antoine much earlier that day, a day that felt like three hundred days of continuous root canals without Novocain and an extra month of colonoscopies added on for good measure. Sean realized at that moment that his presence there served several purposes. Sean was a brother, a confidant, a witness, and, most importantly, a priest. What Michael Cloughey had just laid out for his brother was not the confession of a sociopath or a psychopath or a deranged maniac. Sean did not know exactly what psychological or legal term to place on his brother's actions, but he was pretty sure that the one term sitting stationary in his head fit rather perfectly: confession. The only thing worse than the life actions and choices Michael now spent discussing was the single unifying motive for all the actions.

Sean had no idea what to say. He could have sat on that damned bucket for years and all his brain and mouth would and could agree upon was "Why?" He wanted to be profound and say something to make his brother's visible torment go away. He wanted to be the priest and offer up something inspirational and accept this confession with grace, clarity, and austerity. He was handcuffed, and he couldn't be a brother or a priest or a friend. At that moment, in that shared space, all two hundred and thirty pounds of Sean Cloughey was an observer of an event that was many broken bones and many years in the making.

"You know, I have asked myself why so many times. Yah asked me, Dad asked me, Lara asked, and even Lara's father asked me, and I have never been able to give anyone a reason as to why I have this inside of me. I have specific reasons for certain actions throughout my life, as I told you, but there is something inside of me that fucking hates people. I just hate people, and when they give me even the slightest reason to act against them, I do. I judge everyone. I always have. I feel justified in a sense. People see me and they see frailty, and their supposition is that I am weak. I use that as motivation. I use that idea against them. I wish I could sit here, Sean, and tell you that I don't enjoy physically harming them, but I do. I understand what it does to everyone else I care about. I saw what it did to our parents. I have seen what it has done to Lara, which is why I can't even think about telling her what happened this morning. I know that what I am is the reason why we haven't spoken for years. I am sorry for all of that, but I'm not truly sorry for what I have done to those people. I know what that defines me as, but I honestly don't know if I care. I don't know how to be something else. I don't know how to understand and forgive and compromise. I am an animal that is capable of some feeling and love, but I would rather destroy than understand the simplistic motivations of people who see me and see nothing and then act toward me as though I am some piece of garbage in the street."

Sean took a deep breath, hoping he would be able to absorb at least some of what was on this plate before him. He spoke slowly so as to process all of this. His cadence was more for him than his brother.

"But, Michael, if everyone did this, what would we have? Where would we all be? You sound like you want to be God here and have the right to evaluate everyone's actions, and if you determine that they need to have their face smashed in, then so be it? I could see frustration and anger and resentment as normal human responses to situations. We all feel these things and live these things at times as each and every day passes. It is part of our humanity."

The priest was out and now the pastor was following in line.

"You are not the evaluator of humanity, and you have absolutely no right, no matter how someone 'sees you,' to be violent against them. Do you think this makes you bigger than them or stronger? You will always be five feet and six inches tall, and you will never be much bigger than one hundred and fifty pounds. So, if someone looks at you in the street, you feel the need and the right to rip their head off? This is what you are. Why is that not all right, not enough? Oh, and honestly, don't compare yourself to an animal, Michael. Animals kill out of instinct, hunger, territory, necessity even. With all you have told me today, let me ask you this—have you ever killed anyone? Tell me the truth."

Sean braced himself for the response of yes using the philosophy of pray for the best and expect the worst.

"No. I've wanted to."

"When? Wait…it doesn't matter."

The conversation was not going quite according to Michael's plan, although he wasn't sure he even had one. It just felt wrong. He was alone in the ocean, and his flotation device was asking him why he even got on the boat in the first place. Part of Sean wanted to console his brother and offer up support despite the tremendous and terrible root that had burrowed deep and dark down inside his brother. However, there was another part of Sean that understood this needed to be said to Michael directly. Michael had yet to meet someone who was able to deal with the tenacious anger and absolutely vicious beatings that he was able to distribute with relative ease and apparent enjoyment. But what if one day he met someone who could withstand it, and what if they were able to offer up a ferocity just as terrible? Perhaps even worse? Sean understood what this meant, and he immediately forced himself to stop thinking about it.

"But what do we do with people that do these things, Sean? I should just let them get the best of me and walk away? I should just let guys who throw women out of cars get away with it? I should just let two brothers try to kill me because I fucked their sister? I should have just let Dave mock me on the field that day and run around the bases? And this morning I should have just let this kid put photoshopped pictures of you sucking a dick on his—?"

And like that, it was all over. Every bit of it was over. It was said, and it could not be unsaid ever again by anyone. If it were the movies, music would have started playing or an ominous thunderclap would have struck somewhere.

"Fuck."

CHAPTER 28

IT TOOK ANYA ALMOST TWO HOURS TO FIGURE OUT who the man on Stanley Antoine's phone was. There were several pictures of this guy with rather crude drawings and representations of anal and oral sex. There were no distinguishing features of the pictures nor any identifying marks that provided assistance. Anya took the amount of time both as a challenge to her overall skillset as well as a personal insult. During this time, Robert had called her four times, and each call represented another level of frustration and tension and nerves. This tension was compounded by the phone call Robert had received from DiNardi, who had informed him that a message had been left for him from a reporter. The message was from a Margaret Nieves, and she was the *Daily News's* lead education reporter. The small white message receipt had only her name, place of business, and contact number. The message portion read only "Re: The Events of the Day."

"Fucking Ralph," Robert said as he ended his call with the principal.

Anya entered his office, uncertain if she should smile.

"It fucking took you long enough. I'm embarrassed by the amount of time this took you. I mean, I'm embarrassed for you and for the fact that I continue to employ you even with your shoddy performance and shocking lack of results."

"Eff you." This was code that did not need deciphering. "Do you want to know what's on the phone or not?"

"No. Keep it a secret, Anya. It will be great for when the reporter that just called Ralph gets a hold of all this information and puts it in the fucking newspaper and we end up either in prison or dead somewhere. I don't think I have to remind someone of your intelligence just how significant this school is to the members of this board or how important it is to their interests that this whole fucking mess goes the fuck away. So, pardon me if I seem a little curt. I have the money to get out of the country, but a woman who looks like you usually ends up eating a lot of pussy in prison. For now, just be my assistant and tell me what the fuck is on this kid's phone."

"What reporter?"

"One of those fucking kids called the motherfucking newspaper, and they must have told them that their tiny white English teacher beat the fuck out of a black kid who is the size of a fucking condominium, and she is just a little bit curious if it should be the lead on tonight's news and on every fucking newspaper in the morning and on every social media stream. What is on the fucking phone?"

"Shit, okay. Well, there really isn't much on this kid's phone. He is kind of a bore actually. However…" She leaned forward and placed the phone on the desk in front of Robert.

His eyes opened wide as he rapidly swiped through the pictures. "Please tell me you know who the fuck that is."

She nodded. "That is Pastor Sean Cloughey."

"Wait…"

"Yep. Pastor Sean Cloughey is Michael Cloughey's bother. He is the pastor of St. Sebastian Church."

"Wait…"

"Yep. Stanley Antoine had a whole bunch of photoshopped pictures of Michael Cloughey's brother, who is a *pastor* of a parish, simulating acts of homosexuality on his phone."

"Hold on…"

"I have no idea why. Nothing else on his phone seems to jive with any of this at all. I know he hated his teacher because his grades in the class jeopardized his playing status at times. Aside from these pictures, there is just ridiculous teenage bullshit stuff. Nothing to write home about at all."

"So does Stanley…?" Hanover made a gesture with his two index fingers indicating a connection.

"Nope. There is no evidence I discovered to point to the fact that Stanley has ever even come in contact with the pastor."

Robert put his hand straight up in front of him so that the palm of it was close to Anya's face. She understood his desire for her to stop speaking. She loved to beat him to the punch and finish his sentences. She felt empowered by the ability to know exactly what he was going to ask and how he was going to phrase it. She also understood that the ice of this situation was as thin as ice gets before the person standing on it inevitably found themselves in the most frigid water imaginable. Now was not the time for any kind or type of competition. They needed to rally and rally quickly to figure out what was happening and why, and it all needed to be deduced before Ms.

Nieves from the *News* was able to get any more information than she already probably possessed.

"I'm sorry."

Robert disregarded her apology. He lowered his hand and picked up the cell phone. He handed the cell phone to Anya with his right hand and picked up his desk phone with his left. He placed the desk phone receiver against his chest. Robert looked directly at Anya, and he gave her two direct orders. Although the orders were short and lacking a customary code, the tone in which they were provided might as well have been paragraphs.

"Get DiNardi here and locate Michael Cloughey."

CHAPTER 29

Sean sat next to Michael, feeling a combination of emotions that ranged from a deep sadness to pity to guilt. For a moment, he understood his brother's rage and perhaps a fraction of what constructed him. He felt a sadness that these pictures, pictures of him, had been given life and that they resided in someone's phone. He felt guilty, not for his life, but for somehow playing a small part in his brother's predicament. His faith told him that he needed to find exactly where God resided in this situation. What challenge was God posing here? What needed to be discovered? Was this event a necessary calling together of two estranged brothers who, until this morning, had not spoken in years and who had basically written one another off for living two lives that had no form of connectivity or intersection? So what exactly was he being forced to realize and how was any of it going to play out? Sean was smart enough to understand the apathetic nature of teenagers and how the teenage mind did not always make the connections regarding cruelty of action and the possible outcomes of those actions. Sean thought of Donald Tressell and their conversation regarding technology, morality, and the failings of humanity to be able to homogenize the two within a cold world. How fitting that conversation was considering the circumstances that lay in front of the Cloughey brothers today.

Michael spoke with affirmation. "The Antoine kid today wasn't the only one."

"What are you talking about?"

"Antoine had pictures of you in his phone he manipulated with some software that—"

"Yes, we established that, but what did you mean he wasn't the only one?"

"He wasn't the only one I beat the shit out of."

"Michael, I am aware that you have physically beaten the shit out of a small city's worth of people in your life. I am actually one of them, remember? However, there is something you're not telling me, something you're withholding here. I'll be honest with you. I feel bad for you, and I wish I could tell you what to do and give you some advice and some guidance in a big brother sort of way, but there is also a part of me that feels—and God have mercy on me for saying this—that you're getting what you deserve. However, the call today, the way you look, and how you sound is not you. You usually do something like this and then can easily sit down at the dinner table, roll up your sleeves, and pass the vegetables. You say you hate people and that you feel the need to right the wrongs of the world. There is something perversely noble about the fact that you feel hatred for people who do horrible things. But you are one of those people. You have always—"

"When Dave was rounding first base, he threw me a kiss, remember? It was because of you. It wasn't because of the hit. He always had something cute to say. Right before the game started, he walked over to me and said, 'Hey, Cloughey, after we kick the shit out of you today in front of all these scouts, I'll come by your house later and take your brother out so I can fuck him too.' Before I gave Chris his beating, he walked up to me and whispered a delightful comment about you right in my fucking ear. I didn't kick the shit out of him there because I had a team full of little kids staring at me. The brothers caught their beating because as I was trying to get away from them, one of those assholes said, 'You should try being more like your faggot brother—'"

"Stop, Michael, stop."

Michael sat up straight and looked at the gray sky above him and willed it blue. He took a deep breath and he stood up. He put both hands to his face and wiped down toward his neck. He wished for a split second that he was Sean, but when he moved his hands from his face, he was still him.

"There were others. There have been others in the past. A few. I…I'm sorry, Sean. I'm sorry I'm subjecting you to this. I'm sorry I am your bother. Everyone in my life deserves better than me, than what they have ever gotten. Dad and Yah deserved some peace, you deserved a brother that you weren't afraid of, and Lara and the baby deserve a husband and a father who knows how to enjoy life, who isn't…like this." With the final two words, he opened his hands as if to offer up himself, a bad present that you receive and must disguise your real sentiment of disappointment about.

"Michael, I never—"

"Don't."

Michael looked straight into his brother's eyes for the first time since they were teenagers. He was without expression on his face, and his body felt a sensation he could have only described as giving up. He could tell that Sean was close to tears, and he did not have the desire to be a witness to that event. He had made a lot of people cry.

Michael began unrolling his sleeves to button the cuffs. Ever since he received First Communion and Yah had bought him an actual dress shirt, he always had to have two extra buttons added because his wrists were so thin.

"We are what we are, Sean. We are what God made us, right? If there were no devils, why would we need angels?"

"Why am I here, Michael? Why did you call me today?" Sean closed his eyes and massaged the bridge of his nose with his thumb and forefinger.

"Confession. You're a priest, right?"

Sean smiled wryly and chortled slightly. A moment of guilt struck him suddenly, and he looked up at Michael to confirm that he was truly joking. Once he saw Michael's half smile, he knew his reaction was what was expected. He could not believe Michael had it in him to even attempt a joke, let alone one aligned with the very thoughts in Sean's head. Michael was never one to bust a gut laughing. The most you ever got from him was a short smile or a hint of teeth. A serious look claimed ownership over Michael's face most of the time. It matched his tense body language and the rise of his shoulders. This all gave the illusion that Michael was always uptight or angry. While most of the time that was true, much of the view could be attributed to the fact that the guy just rarely ever laughed or seemed to be happy. Lara was the only one who could ever get Michael to let his shoulders relax and his jaw to loosen. When he was around her, he was somewhat unrecognizable. His eyebrows and forehead, which were always furrowed to the point of leaving lines on his face well into his sleep, would round out and soften, and he even appeared younger.

Sean supposed it was his brother's intensity that made him appealing to women. He knew it wasn't his wit or his lighthearted sense of humor. Lara brought the actual human out of Michael, and Sean supposed that was why he loved her the way he always had. What Sean also knew that Lara did not know was that the entire Cloughey family worshipped her for that. Yah and John Sr. were indebted to Lara for her power. No other person gracing this planet was able to transform their son from a pit bull into a basset hound. All it ever took from Lara was a quick sleepy-eyed look, a hand hold, or, when things were very intense, a short shout of "Cloughey!" Any of these things would return Michael back to a state of Zen. Sean would occasionally laugh to himself and wonder how different both of their lives would have been had those playground swings never existed.

Michael sighed. "We all have to be somewhere, Sean. At some point, we all must look at what we have made of our lives and either fight it or say, ok, this is where I am, where I stand. I am wired this way, and I must be this thing. I thought of you and Lara, and I just had to talk to someone. My supposition is that I am nowhere near strong enough to tell her any of this."

"She knows who her husband is."

"How much more can I ask of her?"

A part of Sean Cloughey wanted to run away and have nothing to do with any more of his brother. Any individual as capable of violence as Michael deserved to be in a place where he couldn't hurt anyone anymore, whether it be in self-defense or in defense of his brother's name and reputation. He knew that Michael did not deserve someone like Lara. Yet there was also another part of Sean that wanted to embrace his brother and simply thank him for putting fist to flesh on his behalf. It was perverse to say it, but it delivered the message that Michael did truly love him all these years. Defending him was a noble thing that almost got him locked up, beaten, and it had left his baseball career in ruins. The priest in him was filled with condemnation, and the brother in him felt like telling the world, "If you want to fuck with one of us, you're going to have to go through both of us." One thing Sean was certain of was Michael's thought concerning his wife. He simply had no idea just how much more Lara Cloughey could handle.

Michael began to stand up, and Sean realized it was time to relinquish his milk crate. He brushed off the back of his pants and felt his phone vibrate in his pocket.

"Hello. This is Father—"

"I know who this is. I called you. I am calling you because your brother's phone is off, and it is essential that a message be delivered to him immediately."

"Who is this?"

"That is not the significant part of this phone call, Father. What *is* significant is that he is asked to report to his place of employment in one hour from now." The woman's voice was professional and curt. It lacked fluctuation in tone and thus made it impossible to detect an origin. This woman could be thirty years old or sixty. She could be white, Hispanic, or African American. He didn't even know why that mattered.

"Well, I am not sure if I can get him this message. I have not spoken to him in quite a few years."

Michael did the furrowed eyebrow thing, and he looked from Sean to his phone. As late day was turning into early evening, he realized that his battery had died.

"I don't know if I will be able to get in contact. What is this in regard—"

"I am sure you will find a way."

The voice was gone, and Sean was left holding his phone.

Michael replied with "Who was that?"

"I have no idea; she wouldn't identify herself. You have to charge your phone. You will be receiving further directions in an hour."

"Why wouldn't she identify herself?"

"I have a better question for you, Michael. How did she know to call me? Only you knew I was coming here, and how did she obtain my phone number?"

Michael looked at his brother, knowing he had no answer to his question. This entire day was already disturbing, but now it was becoming something out of a movie.

"We now have less than one hour to figure out exactly what is going on here, Michael."

CHAPTER 30

ST. CATHERINE'S PREPARATORY SCHOOL OPENED ITS
doors in the fall of 1942. It was founded by Mr. Walter P.
Simmins and his energetic and much younger wife, Bernadette.
This age gap did not escape the press, and it certainly did not
escape the scuttlebutt of the wealthy circles of the Northeast
Corridor of the United States. Walter Simmins was the owner
of the Simmins Steel Company, originally located in Edinboro,
Pennsylvania. The Simmins family at large resided in the Erie
Valley and the outlying territory stretching south to Akron,
Ohio, and as far east, past the Susquehannock State Forest to
Scranton. This would become known as the Simmins Triangle
by many who had entertained a business stay in that region as
early as the middle to late 1880s and on. The Simmins family
did not need steel to make them as ridiculously wealthy as they
were, but it sure did put three cherries on top of the ice cream
sundae that was already covered in hot fudge and an obscene

amount of whipped cream. While steelmaking was the legitimate branch of the family business, they amassed quite a large bit of wealth bootlegging vast amounts of alcohol from New York through the Erie Valley waterways and on to Detroit. That alcohol would then find its way to Chicago before making a sharp left and heading down south to Tennessee. It then made its penultimate stop on this scenic journey in the safe and capable arms of the Florida rumrunners who had the boats and means to transport some of the finest rum the world had ever seen in Cuba. The steel industry came readily equipped with manufacturing plants, large convoys of trucks, and plenty of manpower to make sure every bottle was escorted safe and sound to its rightful owner. Walter was also a large fan at hiding things in plain sight, and the point of origin for most of the alcohol being swiftly transported by the enormous black and gold trucks of the Simmins Steel Company was New York City. It was no surprise that the individuals responsible for a good amount of that business were also responsible for the boom in real estate and industrialization, especially around the waterways of New York City. The East River of New York had undergone massive changes with the construction of the Brooklyn Bridge in the late 1880s and Manhattan Bridge in the early 1900s. If industrialization had not been enough to add to the coffers of the Simmins Steel Company, there were always the numerous contracts that the government issued for steel production during the early years of World War II. It came as little to no surprise to companies that had put massive bids in for this work that the contracts for the manufacture of steel for many of these projects were given to the highly dependable and well-respected Simmins family. Bernadette Simmins family, the Utlands, longtime residents of Sleepy Hollow, New York, of

Ichabod Crane fame, were extremely well thought of through-out the Upstate New York region, and they had their hand on the pulse of many of the power players of the New York political scene. In truth, most of the deals that favored Walter's efforts were made over seven-course dinner engagements and committed to Simmins Steel well prior to ever seeing the oblig-atory light of day as ruled over by business practices.

As Simmins Steel concluded its lucrative and time-consum-ing commitment to the bridges, Bernadette got the itch to truly settle down, adopt a real suburban lifestyle, and have children close to her childhood home. As Walter and Bernadette had their third child, the roar of the '20s had devolved into a low purr and the world did an absolute somersault. Be it the guilt of living the way they had, remorse for their contributions to illegality, their corrupt entanglements, or the now growing children around her, Bernadette begged her husband to build a home and school for the underserved children of the Depression. Bernadette's parents had passed shortly after the birth of their first grandson and were buried in the most sought-after and prestigious burial ground on the East Coast of the United States, Greenwood Cemetery. Walter fell in love with Greenwood Cemetery, not because he adored his in-laws or because he loved what Richard Upjohn and David Douglass had done with their allotment of 478 acres of land. Truth be told, he fervently disliked his in-laws despite their efforts to curry business consistently and successfully in his favor, and he had no actual idea who Upjohn and Douglass were. No, Walter Simmins loved Greenwood Cemetery simply because, in the right location and at its highest elevations, you could gaze longingly at the sturdy steel his company had crafted and hand-somely given over to the Brooklyn and Manhattan Bridges. As Bernadette and Walter sat in repose on a stone carved bench in the cemetery on a beautiful, clear morning in the spring of 1939, Bernadette convinced her husband to purchase a small parcel of land in which they would construct a school with a large home. The entire institution would be neatly placed between Greenwood Cemetery and Prospect Park in the neighborhood quaintly entitled Windsor Terrace Brooklyn. Walter's company bought the land from a desperately bankrupt farmer, Dennis Grimley, and they utilized most of the area primarily used for stables and several carriage houses to convert into the actual school building itself. With an incredibly sturdy foundation in place, the construction of the large building took little to no time at all, and when you had the committed and highly focused mind of Walter Simmins working toward a goal, things normally got done. If they did not, well, then God help the individuals responsible for any form of delay, even if it be caused by Mother Nature herself.

By late September of 1942, St. Catherine's Preparatory School was completed. Bernadette chose to name the school after Saint Catherine of Alexandria. As a little girl, Bernadette's father told her the story of the fourteen-year-old girl who was responsible for converting hundreds of individuals to Christianity and was martyred only a few short years later for doing so. It was also said that Joan of Arc identified St. Catherine as one of the saints who offered her counsel during her most trying ordeals. Bernadette thought Saint Catherine would be the perfect role model for young men and women in need of guidance, education, and a new start to their young lives.

The ribbon-cutting ceremony of St. Catherine's was attended by some of the most esteemed members of the New York social scene, and they all attended with checks containing numerous zeros. The zeros served two purposes. The first was a conscious and purely unadulterated competition, wealthy families vying for their family name to be plastered on things such as a library or lecture halls or landmarks. The second and more truthful purpose was to relieve guilt. The wealthy elite of New York never admitted being or feeling guilty about the vast amounts of money they possessed. They stuck to their social circles, competed, and accumulated more as each generation rolled by. However, contrary to what was displayed externally, many in the upper echelon of these wealthy families held on to a very deep-seated guilt. Whether it was the overwhelming and noticeable disparity in class, the illegal means by which their wealth had been amassed, or simply being able to indulge in an ostentatious lifestyle while many around them were in bread lines, there resided in many a true sense of guilt. This guilt was the cause of many things. In some, it manifested itself in contributions to enormous building projects. In others, it caused large contributions to the arts, and in others, it caused an aggressive display of plastering their family name on anything they saw that caught their eye. For others, this vast wealth created a sense of ennui, and for the more forlorn, melancholy.

Whatever the cause, reason, motivation, or desire, Walter and Bernadette ended the day with enough money to name two libraries, seven lecture halls, a theatre, a baseball field, and several campus landmarks. What finances remained after all that work was completed would be placed handsomely aside for an endowment that would act as one of the largest academic endowments this side of anywhere. Not only would Bernadette see her dream more than realized, but her brand-new institution, by all accounts in the history books, would be deemed "recession-proof." This was especially comforting given the lessons of the prior twelve years or so.

It was also at this very point that Walter and Bernadette were surprised with their fourth child, a beautiful little girl. While not birthed by Bernadette or of any blood relation, she was the child of one of Walter's most trusted assistants of over twenty years who asked if they would adopt her. If not for their ability to do this and Bernadette's love for children, the girl would have entered into the very foster care system that St. Catherine's tried to protect children from. Thousands of homeless children in New York had begun flooding the system in the mid to late 1800s, and the city, the system, and the country seemed ill-equipped to know exactly what to do with them. Foster care became an oxymoron which led to abuse, pain, and neglect. When Bernadette was introduced to the newest member of their family, despite her age, she immediately fell in love with her and latched on as if she had given birth herself after carrying her for nine months. Walter was a little slower in his attachment. He felt done with that part of his life and was not prepared to raise another child. However, as with most things, he deferred to Bernadette's wants. He always, without her knowledge, felt she knew best regarding what made a family. He had a tremendous amount of confidence in her, and he knew, just by how she looked at this child, that she had more love to give. He wanted her to have this, and as the years passed, he never regretted it.

As most if not all institutions are wont to do over the years, St. Catherine's evolved, grew, and expanded in size, scope, and purpose. By the 1950s, enrollment was five hundred and fifty, up from its original opening number of 122. By the early sixties, the school blossomed north of 1,067. This caused a medium-size renovation, eliciting more funding from those who were new to the world of philanthropy while simultaneously drawing back in some old money. The mid to late seventies witnessed another population explosion as New York City's population started booming. St. Catherine's Preparatory High School changed focus and dedicated itself to the arts. This would include a total student enrollment of twenty-seven hundred students, ballet, orchestra, theater programs, and a plethora of literary residents offering insightful readings of their very own work. By the time the 1980s and '90s came around, the school was known as one of the best in the country, and the well over three thousand students regularly moved on to elite Ivy League colleges and undertook residences in some of the larger banking and finance companies. Money coming in was now dedicated to massive endowments and scholarships for academics, the arts and sciences, and, of course, sports.

Walter Simmins had passed in the winter of 1961 after a lengthy battle with pneumonia. He had become more immersed in the school as he grew older, forcing him to pull away from business when he just could not physically or mentally contribute to the day-to-day operations and finances. The Simmins Steel Company would continue to thrive under the guidance and highly stable leadership of his eldest son, David. Bernadette Simmins lived to the age of ninety-seven. It was not until she turned ninety-four that she began to show her age. Dementia grabbed hold of Bernadette and worked incredibly quickly. She passed as daintily as she lived her life, asleep in the bed that she had shared with her husband for decades. David eulogized his mother alongside his siblings, Abagail, Marie, Connor, and Dorothy. He called her a true pioneer in the world of education and an incredibly devoted wife, mother, and grandmother. Walter and Bernadette would have seventeen grandchildren, and almost all were present to see their grandmother entombed alongside their grandfather, the legendary Walter, in their family mausoleum erected on Wisteria Path in Greenwood Cemetery. Shortly after Walter's passing, she had a stone bench placed beside the mausoleum where she would sit and talk to her husband. The bench was dedicated to her parents, the Utlands. Bernadette did this as a purposeful yet slightly playful jab at her husband. She would often sit on this bench during the warmer months and read Walter various articles from the *New York Times* that she believed he would find of interest. When she was done reading the paper, Bernadette would take off her reading glasses and stare out at a clearing of trees in the distance. The placement of the family mausoleum on Wisteria Path was not an accident, nor was the placement of the Utland bench. Wisteria Path was located on Battle Hill in Brooklyn. It was the sight of the largest and one of the most significant battles of the American Revolutionary. Battle Hill was the highest point in Brooklyn at 216 feet above sea level. The clearing of trees that Bernadette would gaze through, some days with sadness and other days with nostalgia, offered up a perfect view of the now very crowded and awe-inspiring New York skyline. Regardless of the foliage, this view also offered up pristine views of both the Brooklyn and Manhattan Bridges. Before straining to stand in later years, Bernadette from time to time would say clearly and proudly, "Look at what you made, Walt. Just look."

By 1994, St. Catherine's Preparatory School would be called St. Catherine's Preparatory Academy, and it would give itself over to a new board structure that came equipped with a thirty-six-member board of trustees. This board would continue the work that the Simmins family had started many, many years prior to their birth, and they would continue to increase the endowments, scholarships, and offerings of the school. By this point in time, David Simmins's middle daughter, Maureen Simmins, was one of the ex officio caretakers of the school. Her foundation, Simmins Trust, dedicated itself to many philanthropic pursuits ranging from education to cancer research to military veteran rehabilitation. Maureen was tall and strikingly beautiful. Some would say she was all the best parts of a highly attractive Simmins and Utland gene tree. She spoke three languages, was educated at Princeton University, and she held two doctorate degrees, one in theology and the other in sociology. She developed a true appreciation in theology as a child when her grandmother would tell her the stories of Joan of Arc, St. Catherine, and, her favorite, David and Goliath. That David inspired the name of her father, whom she adored with every bit of her being.

Maureen always struck an immediate response from most individuals in any and every room she entered. Her husband would often say that she was so pretty she would even turn heads before walking into the room. The Simmins family name still held more than great weight in New York City as well as most of the Northeast. They were one of the wealthiest families in the country, and they had managed to do what some other wealthy families had not, combine old and new money. They did this in one fell swoop in the early spring of 2002. A year earlier, while vacationing on the Amalfi Coast, Maureen was sitting at a café with two of her dearest friends. Most men found her beauty intimidating, and they would often shy away from making advances or even striking up conversation. She was the rare beautiful and equally smart woman who just could not get a date or find a mate who could compete with her step for step. Her friends even stopped trying to set her up with some of New York City's most eligible bachelors because it had always ended in a highly unsuccessful story. On that specific day at that café, she was approached by a rather handsome, well-dressed, and incredibly well-spoken man. The fact that he had walked over to her table while addressing her in perfectly spoken Italian and holding an enormous yellow rose was not the most memorable part of their introduction that afternoon. It was the fact that he was accompanied by a full musical ensemble consisting of a five-member consort of string musicians playing "La Canzone del Sole," the "Song of the Sun." While he spoke to her, crowds of natives and tourists gathered to observe who this man and these musicians were dedicating this much energy to. When he presented his rose and asked for her hand and permission to dance, several in the crowd placed their hands over their mouths because the sheer romantic presence of the scene caused this immediate and captivating response.

When the song slowed, he asked her name, to which she replied, "Maureen Ophelia Simmins of New York City." He smiled a broad smile that was slightly crooked and favored the left side of his face. She immediately liked this smile because it also displayed a single dimple. The dimple played nicely with the strong jaw and the strength of his chin. It also did not hurt that he had light green eyes that could be mistaken for a gray color under the right circumstances of light. He stated that he was also from New York City, had heard her name before, and seen her in many newspapers. He also explained that he simply never had the joyous opportunity to make her acquaintance in the busier and often impersonal New York social scene until this moment and more than four thousand miles away. He explained that this moment was fated to occur and that he would be beyond honored if she would accompany him to dinner later that evening. He informed her that their dinner would be attended solely by them. He assured her with a now coy smile that the musicians would be left at his hotel.

Maureen was immediately captivated, and whether it was the heat of the afternoon or the proximity to this incredibly charming man, she felt a slight flush of excitement throughout her legs and the hand he was holding. She had almost forgotten that they were still dancing slowly while being surrounded by a healthy swarm of people. She responded with "*Sì*," and she tilted her head to the side to return his coy smile with a shy smile that spoke hundreds of words in one moment. He asked for her number and the hotel where she was staying with her friends. As they ended their dance, the crowd, now practically weeping, began to cheer and applaud. He held her hand high in the air, and she offered everyone a polite and sincere curtsy. He gestured with both of his hands in her direction as if to direct all the applause toward her, and she felt her face become warm from the attention. He applauded Maureen and leaned in close to her right ear to inform her that he would meet her at eight. As he broke their shared gaze and his proximity to turn and walk away, she stopped him by placing her hand on his shoulder.

"I'm so sorry. Our viewing audience must have distracted me and my manners. I never asked your name."

He smiled that slightly crooked smile again and placed his hand on his chest while looking down. When his eyes returned to meet hers, he replied.

"I should be the one apologizing. My name is Robert. Robert Hanover."

A year to the day later, Robert Hanover and Maureen Ophelia Simmins were married, and her old money mixed with his burgeoning success and new money combined to make them one of the wealthiest and most entertaining couples in the United States. Shortly after they were married and returned from their one-month honeymoon, Robert Hanover filled the vacant board chair position at St. Catherine's Preparatory Academy. At first, he did this as an act of pure selflessness and true gravitas. Maureen Hanover-Simmins had asked, and he jumped. Jumping at her beckoning was something Robert did most readily during the very early years of their marriage. The Hanover-Simmins merger was a thing of acclaim, and his affiliation with the institution would being attention, wealth, and a flurry of new board representation. That new representation would be best represented with pockets as deep as Hudson River. Robert did his part; he filled the board with up-and-coming men and women of financial esteem. They were either part of his financial circle from his earlier years in banking and financial advising or they were friends of those friends.

What Robert Hanover had realized in the very embryonic phase of his board chairmanship was that schools of any size, shape, and scope were incredible places to garner and gather the interest of wealthy individuals. If it so happened that some of those individuals and their wealth had come from illicit means, then so be it. If it happened that some of the wealth belonging to friends also needed to be hidden or "cleaned," then so be it. And if it happened that some of the money being cleaned or washed or scrubbed several times over was being done so through phony construction projects, scholarships for students that did not exist or were never given anywhere except on paper, or even in endowments that were earmarked in the name of deceased family members, then so be that as well.

Robert Hanover, without the knowledge or consent of his strikingly beautiful wife, had succeeded in turning St. Catherine's into a full-fledged money laundering business. It worked flawlessly. Robert would admit to Anya that no one would ever doubt the true and honorable St. Catherine's Prep

Academy, given their lineage, and no one would ever question the vast amounts of wealth being poured into an already wealthy institution. It was hiding dirty money in plain sight, and he was more than happy to do it. He even chuckled when he told her that the school was built on the very bedrock of dirty money from Walter Simmins and his bootlegging counterparts of decades past. It was as if this is where this type of money should always come home to reside. Robert filled the finance offices of St. Catherine's with his people, and the school ran efficiently, effectively, and above reproach as one of the finest academic institutions in the country while simultaneously functioning to clean money from every ill-gotten means vetted by both him and his trustworthy assistant now sitting across his desk. Until that morning the school, the business, the con, and the palm lining had gone on without so much as a hiccup. This morning Robert Hanover was introduced to the worst case of hiccups he had ever encountered. However, this case of hiccups came packaged in a very small and highly underestimated package, and its name was Michael Cloughey. Mr. Cloughey, without knowing it, was causing quite a stir because he punched a student roughly three times his size at the very place that the media was now asking questions about. This was not the publicity he wanted, and he knew the minute that the events of this morning hit the news cycle, he would have to answer to some incredibly powerful, intimidating, and potentially horrifying people. Robert Hanover was starting to get the sense of what it felt like to be Headmaster DiNardi.

CHAPTER 31

MICHAEL ARRIVED HOME WITH SEAN AND FOUND IT empty and dark. They had walked through that same door together so many times, but today it felt like a different door attached to a different house in a different city. Michael and Lara had moved everything into his childhood home when things began getting very cloudy and distant for John Sr. Lara urged Michael to make the move even though he was highly resistant at first. He explained that he wanted a place that was theirs and theirs alone. With a little boy running around and Lara in "contract negotiations" with him about a second child, it proved difficult to find an apartment that could accommodate their need for space as well as their budget. Michael would often tell realtors to suspend their amazement at the fact that a high school English teacher was not making a small fortune. In fact, Lara made a significant amount more than Michael did working for a fast-growing interior design firm. She was very good at what she did, and she was always being recognized as the first introduction that the CEO and COO of Avalon Design would make when courting a new client. Her interior design style was very much like her fashion sense. Understated with clean lines and incredibly sophisticated color choices. She could be bold if her client demanded it, but she preferred to let the room embrace you and demand you to stay and appreciate it. For Lara, design was always about adapting to your surroundings while remaining in full control of them—not an easy feat to pull off by a young designer. Her education was impressive, her experience was evolving, and her ability to gain the trust of even the largest of clients was remarkable.

In the very early stages of her career, she was given the design for a musician's rather unnecessarily large home in the Hamptons. She met with him and gathered a sense of who he was and what he was looking for. He proved difficult, elusive, and ever resistant to committing to a design choice. The more she pressed, the more he pulled away and the harder he became to contact on the road. His agent was of no assistance, and his personal assistant was more actively engaged with writing his manuscript than with his home. Lara spent days at a time with swatches, design palettes, and vision boards, and she even listened to his music repeatedly to get a sense of the man. Michael found her asleep in front of her computer one night with the baby resting on her chest and an entire room of multicolored Post-it notes with ideas, words, thoughts, and quotes on them, a combination of brainstorming session and late-night detective work on serial killer motivation. Michael loved this scene. He loved seeing her with their son pressed against her, the two things he loved the most softly illuminated by the glow of the computer screen. Two people he would give everything he had for. Two people he felt he didn't deserve. But here they were with him on this ride, and he knew he had to give them more than just a one-and-a-half-bedroom apartment in which every inch of the eight hundred square feet of space was occupied. Knowing his father needed assistance and care greater than he could provide, he charted a course to secure a live-in facility that had all that John Sr. could ask for. Lara and Michael packed up and moved into the house, and the rather excessive rent they were paying for their tiny apartment went to the monthly payments for Millennium Housing, a full-service health care and living facility.

Right before they moved in to the Cloughey house, Lara had completed the house in the Hamptons by going the ultimate minimalist route. She had everything painted white, furnished the entire home with white furniture, cabinets, draperies, and the faintest of bamboo flooring. The only item that presented and truly showed itself was a black Steinway Model O living room grand piano. Her firm, three magazines, numerous colleagues, and her road musician client called it "inspired, breathtaking, and visionary." She was interviewed and asked questions about her inspiration and design ideas. Lara thought of a very design-oriented and elaborate response to fill their articles. Michael looked at the design and laughed at the articles. She got irritated at his response.

"What is so funny to you? You've never decorated a room or designed anything in your life."

"Babe."

"What?"

"You painted a room white. C'mon." He smirked.

"Is Michael upset and jealous that his wife is in magazines, and no one has interviewed him about how he teaches *The Sun Also Rises*?"

She got closer to him, and he put his hands up to protect against a jab at his ribcage from her tiny hands. They were both smirking now.

"You know, you might have been in *Sports Illustrated* if you hadn't decided to lose your shit on a baseball field once."

She could feel the very large dart she just threw at her husband hit him in four places. His face abandoned the smirk that once held residence, and his shoulders dropped simultaneously with his sigh.

"Too soon, Mr. Cloughey?"

"You absolutely know I hate when—"

"Michael, you know the only thing worse than a man who doesn't know when his wife is making a joke?"

Michael tilted his head to the side.

"A man who has no idea that his wife wants him to fuck her because she has a fresh mouth."

An hour and a half later, they were lying in bed together with their legs intertwined and the comforter covering them in the sparsest of ways while the smell of her perfume, their sweat, and body heat filled the room.

"Do you still want to know where I came up with the design?"

Her head was on his chest. His right hand was caressing her shoulder, and the fingers of his left hand were tracing their way up and down her thigh that was atop his waist.

"I don't know, Ms. Trammell. Are you sure you won't have to kill me if you tell me the creative secrets of an interior designer?"

Fully exposed with his hands paying her all the attention, she was able this time to get her tight, controlled jab to hit home in his ribcage. Michael blew out a full breath and closed his eyes to let it pass.

"Well done, Lara. Sure, tell me."

"From two things. First, every 'important' person wants to feel as if they are the most important thing in every room they are in. He plays the piano—it's his piano. His house, it's him. He will always stand out and be the most important thing there."

"Smart. I quite like that. Play to the ego. What's the other thing?"

"The baby."

"What? What baby?"

"Our baby, dummy."

She sat up and looked at him propped up on one arm, naked. She leaned into him as if she were uttering a secret of severe magnitude.

"Daniel's baby chair inspired me. He was sitting in it one day, and I gave him an Oreo cookie. He ate one half and scooped out the filling the way he does to eat it. He likes to leave one half for last, but something caught his attention and he just left it there. The round black cookie just sitting on top of the pure white high chair table just gave me this motivation."

She shrugged and made this little silly face. They both looked at each other and began to laugh uncontrollably at the thought of this and how she had created these grandiose ideas of inspiration when really it all boiled down to the ego and the Oreo.

Michael grabbed her face between both of his hands and kissed her. He looked her in the eyes. "You are the most re-markable woman I will ever be lucky enough to know."

Several weeks later, they moved into his family home, hav-ing made the arrangement that she would be allowed to restore and complete a full design over time, and he would stay out of her way while she engaged in all of this. He agreed.

That was several years ago almost to the day. She had made good on most of her promise to restore the house back to its original prewar features, and Michael made very good on his promise to stay the hell away from anything related to her design or restoration. He did marvel at her work, though. However, Michael had been marveling at Lara from the minute he saw her on a swing at the park many years ago.

Sean looked around at the work Lara had done, and he was filled with emotion and surprise. He had not seen the house, not wanting much to do with it since he left, and he certainly hadn't been invited over for weekly dinners.

"Your wife is an absolute artist, Michael."

Michael wasn't paying attention. He was occupied with turning the lights on and plugging his phone into its charger on his desk. Michael hated this time of the year. He disliked the cold weather, and he disliked when sunset would occur at around 4:30 in the afternoon.

By his phone sat a padded manila envelope next to a note from Lara that read: *Tried your cell. Why do you even have one? Went to get the baby from daycare. Package was hand delivered to you from work. Love you.*

Michael immediately got a terrifyingly cold feeling in his stomach. Who was this package from, and had anyone from the school spoken to Lara about what had gone on that morning? Michael called out Sean's name in a way to illustrate his anxiety. Maybe she knew and she went to get the baby to go to her mother and leave him for good. Michael started sweating again. Sean came into the living room, still overwhelmed at the work done on the house.

"You know, she even restored the molding in the hallway where Mom used to take our height. She—"

"Sean!"

Michael pointed at the rather stuffed envelope on the desk.

"It's from work. It was hand delivered. Earlier. Lara left it. You don't think she knows?"

Sean walked over to the desk quickly, and he lifted the package with both hands. He looked at both sides to discover no writing of any sort. It had a heft to it. He put it down and picked up Lara's note and read it quietly.

"Michael, your wife has no idea that you struck a child and potentially destroyed your life and career."

"How the fuck do you know that?"

"Because if she knew what you did today, do you think she would leave you a sweet, loving little note like this? Jesus, she even has perfect penmanship."

Michael picked up the package as his phone was returning to life. It began vibrating repeatedly, and he could feel the day playing itself out all over again with each vibration. The screen read, "16 Missed Calls" and "8 Voice Mail Messages."

"I can't open this package."

Sean put down Lara's note and looked around the living room. "Do you have alcohol?"

Michael would not remove his gaze from the package on his desk. "Dining room. Bar cart near the credenza."

"Okay, here's the plan. I want you to take two glasses and pour us two whiskeys and fill half the glass with ice. I then want you to go upstairs and take a shower and change your clothes. I am going to investigate this anonymous delivery. You have fifteen minutes. Go."

Michael stood there and looked at Sean with eyes that he had seen before. They were tired and had very dark circles fixed around them. His hair was matted with sweat, and he had an odor coming off him that let those around him know that his deodorant had taken a sabbatical well prior to his arrival home. Sean remembered this face, minus the gashed knuckles and scratches to Michael's face, from the night he came home after his delightful encounter with the Peterson brothers. Years later and still that face. He had prayed for Michael that night and many nights since. The prayers had not worked. Sean decided not to leave this portion of the evening to God and to take matters into his own hands.

"Michael. Go shower. I believe you will be a getting a phone call, perhaps?"

Michael poured the drinks and placed them on the dining room table and, with an absent personality, walked upstairs.

Sean heard the shower turn on. He took the package to the dining room table and took a seat. He took a large swig from the glass in front of him, and he rolled an ice cube around his mouth. What the alcohol burned; the ice cube extinguished. Sean removed his black-framed reading glasses from his shirt pocket. He rubbed his eyes, wiped the sweat from his forehead, and placed the glasses on his face so they would rest comfortably on the bridge of his nose. He took a deep breath and ripped the top flap from the package to remove the contents. He spread it all out on the table and looked at it and took a healthier sip from his glass, this time with no ice cube chaser. An extremely puzzled look arrived on the face of Sean Cloughey. He leaned forward.

"Who is Vera?"

CHAPTER 32

Michael was given fifteen minutes for his shower, but he took twenty-five. A large portion of him didn't think he would be able to go back downstairs, and he wondered if there was any way he could comfortably live in the bathroom for the rest of his days. It had just about everything you needed to survive, and he was certain that once Lara heard about his day, she would be more than willing to lock him in and slip him food under the door once a day. Much of that, however, was a very large assumption on his part. The locking in he was confident in, but the daily food delivery was more of a long shot. The steam from the shower had dissipated, but the room retained its moisture and humidity. With a large sweep of his forearm, he was able to clear some of the condensation from the mirror, enough to see a portion of himself. He was distorted and misshapen. He leaned in. He was able to catch his eyes looking back, and he held back tears by tightening his jaw and swallowing hard. He knew but still wondered how he had gotten to this specific place, to this moment.

He replayed the morning in his head as if by remote control. He had felt good in the morning, refreshed. Most mornings he woke up to a litany of aches and pains from neck to back to feet. There were days where his stomach didn't feel settled until he was in front of his first period literature class. Michael had a deep-seated love/hate relationship with teaching as there were days he felt as though it was a true calling and where his classes and his delivery flowed like delicious maple syrup. Other days he felt very much outmatched like Officer Ed Tom in one of his favorite novels, *No Country for Old Men*, by Cormac McCarthy, and the day flowed like a brick covered in peanut butter. Technology, social media in particular, was a very worthy adversary for the attention of his students. This morning, social media and technology had thrown a haymaker, and it connected directly to Michael's psyche. It hit more pointedly than any opponent's fist in any street fight he'd ever had. The movie he was playing in his head slowed to him seeing Stanley Antoine turning over his phone and looking up at him to show him the pictures of the man who was sitting downstairs imposed onto some of the most graphic images he had ever seen. His gaze turned from the phone to Stanley's enormous smile and nodding head. The movie replayed him dropping the pile of papers from his hands and him grabbing Stanley's shirt collar near the knot in his tie. He could see Stanley's eyes open to truly question what he was doing. He could feel his fist strike the young man's face in the corner where the jawbone forms its connection. He felt the punch begin in his fist, extend up into his forearm, and explode into his shoulder. Then the movie stopped.

"Who the fuck are you?" Michael asked the distorted shape in the mirror. He had been out of answers for a very long time, and he was pretty sure that no one else had ideas either.

Ten minutes later, he was walking down the staircase to the dining room, and he heard Sean on the phone. His gut tightened at the thought that Sean had fielded the call that was meant for him, but when Sean ended the call with "I owe you one," he realized it was not a call from the mystery voice.

Michael walked into the dining room and saw what amounted to a small office's worth of papers on his dining room table. He saw both glasses he had poured earlier empty as well as the bottle he had poured it from had lost even more of its contents.

Sean heard Michael approaching and he put his phone away. He walked excitedly over to the doorway and had a look on his face that Michael had not been witness to for decades.

"Sean, who was on the phone?"

"A friend. You have got to see this, Mike." Sean hadn't referred to him as Mike since they were young boys. He had always preferred the full Michael. If Sean had used the name Mikey, he would have really thought he had entered another dimension.

"Sean, Lara's going to be here any minute with the baby. What is all of this? What's going on? Why are you excited?"

"Well, at first glance, I believe that this was a package delivered to you with purpose. Who is Vera?"

"Vera?" Michael shrugged as if to ask, given all the circumstances of his current existence, why that was a question at that moment. He wondered if the priest had a hard time holding his liquor.

Sean walked to the far end of the dining room table, he picked up a small piece of notepaper and delivered it, writing side up, to Michael's view. It read, "Vera—646-743-2221."

"Vera Conroy." Michael said her full name with a gasp as if exasperated.

"Yes. Vera Conroy delivered this package to you earlier today. I just hung up from a very quick call with her. She sounded a bit nervous and mousy, but she happens to be on her way over and she would like to shed some light on this."

"I do not believe that I could be any more confused about my life right now."

"Mike, I have no real idea as to what this is all about, but I can tell you that this woman appears to want to help you for some reason. The package that she delivered is filled with names and financial documents and spreadsheets and a litany of material that is above my pay grade. She said she will be here shortly."

"But…What does any of this have to do with what *I* did today, Sean? This morning, I punched a student and was not arrested. I wasn't even asked to write a statement. I was interviewed by the headmaster, who is useless, and I was told by Vera to go home. *You* get an ominous phone call for me, my dining room looks like a copy center threw up, and we are having Vera Conroy over for dinner? What the fuck?"

Michael took a breath and sat down in one of the chairs. He half attempted to look at the papers on the table and half wanted to pass out. He had not eaten since the morning, and he felt shaky and slightly nauseated.

"Well, sit and catch your breath. Vera is on her way over, as well as a friend of mine. He may be able to assist in some capacity. It is nice to have allies. I also ordered two pizzas, by the way. They and our guests should all be here momentarily."

Michael looked up at his brother and placed his head on both of his folded arms on the table. He had desperately wanted his brother back in his life for years, but he could not believe that any of this was now happening and that his brother was in his house and that he was about to host some odd fucking pizza party. He thought that there was absolutely no way that the day could get any more disturbing.

Michael's jerked his head to the side, and he snapped up to a full standing position.

Lara's key was opening the front door.

CHAPTER 33

Robert Hanover's phone had been ringing repeatedly for the last several hours without him answering any number he did not recognize or have stored in contacts. He had only recognized one. Every ring tightened his stomach and created a sense of heightened aggravation.

The last number had called three times but only finally left a message after the last missed call. Robert immediately and loudly called Anya into his office at seeing the voice mail notification. Anya came running into his office as if she were the first on site at a building fire. Her hair was up in a tightened bun atop her head and held in place with a pencil. This was always a sign that she was toiling away. She hated the feeling of her hair falling in front of her face as she was working. Distractions took away valuable seconds and those led to minutes of not being able to produce.

Her mother once had a lengthy discussion of her work life and why she felt this loyalty toward "this Mr. Hanover." Anya could never describe it, and when she tried, she just fell short of the true power and intent of her feelings. It certainly had to do with the incredibly healthy salary she received, and it didn't hurt that she received bonuses, cars, and other perks. If she wanted to go to any event in New York City, it happened. If she wanted to attend Fashion Week or a movie premiere or an impossible to get into sports event or concert, she could, and she could because of Robert Hanover. Anya had everything she could possibly want or hope for until her mother explained to her that she had absolutely very little of what mattered. While she could attend all these incredible events and be a part of these once-in-a-lifetime experiences, she never did. She was always working, always serving the needs of that same Robert Hanover at all hours of the day. She was fiercely loyal because she valued their relationship, but she mostly valued the fact that he challenged every fiber of her being almost every second of the day. She desired that, and she reveled in it, but Anya Crawford needed it to survive. She had never felt the pure pleasure of the hunt or challenge as she had during her years with Robert Hanover. She loved their missions, and she craved the challenges that each of those missions posed. It quenched a thirst that no other relationship could, and if it meant that she would never have time for a relationship or children or to engage in things she had always wanted to do, then so be it. To sit around and weep over those things was an act of weakness, and weeping was another distraction she did not have the time nor the inclination for. And that was the major point of contention that Anya's mother had raised. She would attempt to explain to her daughter that after all the dust settled on a person's life, the only thing they could not reclaim was time. Time was the great equalizer, and it had the longest winning streak known to mankind. Thirty became forty, and forty became sixty, and unlike what Gatsby expressed, you certainly cannot repeat the past or get that time back. Anya would always smile politely and look endearingly at her mother during these conversations while thinking, *Hyperbolize much?* In turn, Anya's mother always came away feeling that she had to keep trying to have these conversations but felt as if talking to a sack of potatoes would lead to greater results.

"Do you know this number?"

"Not at all."

"Fuck."

Robert pressed the voice mail button and sent it to speakerphone.

"Good afternoon, Mr. Hanover. My name is Sarah Nieves. I am a reporter, and I am trying to gather some information regarding St. Catherine's and gain some insight about a possible incident that may have occurred at the school this morning. I was given your name as a point of contact. I await your return call. Thank you for your—"

Robert hung up before Ms. Nieves could finish her polite and professional goodbye. He closed his eyes and looked upward and returned his face to both of his hands so they could vigorously rub his face. One of these days, he was certain to rub the entire front of his face clear off his head.

Robert spoke with a very monotone demeanor, but as he did, he looked slightly down to the left as to not make eye contact with Anya. This was highly unusual for him. He was normally locked into her eyes when discussing anything of importance. They were able to read off one another and perhaps feed off the other's reaction and debate it. But this look suggested that Robert wanted no part of discussion or intellectual discourse whatsoever. Anya had been around for a long time, and she had not seen this Robert Hanover.

"You know, Anya, I have had just about enough of this. This guy is probably sitting at home right now with his feet up having a drink, and we are here fielding a call from this fucking reporter. Too much defense. We need to Tom Brady this shit."

"What's the call?"

"I'm going to have a drink, and we will then call Mr. Michael Cloughey and his priest and find out what we are really up against. That phone call will dictate how the rest of this evening will go. Today has felt like twenty days."

"Want me to call the reporter?"

Robert finally made eye contact. He spoke firmly. "No! Let her twist. Order dinner."

CHAPTER 34

Lara Louise Trammell Cloughey, upon walking into the dining room of the childhood home of the Cloughey family, a room she had yet to fully begun the restoration of, dropped the entirety of the large bag of groceries she had purchased. Her brown leather bag slid off her shoulder, and her Tiffany key ring fell to the floor, making an odd metallic sound. She let go of her son's hand simply because she had lost feeling in her body. She was as frozen as the small bag of green beans that had fallen to the floor. Daniel ran over to hug his father.

"What is this about?"

"Lara, we—"

"Not you, Sean. You. What is actually happening right now?"

She directed her gaze and her words at her husband. In all her years of being a part of the Cloughey family, she had not been in the same room with both Cloughey brothers since the day Sean married them. Even though she kept in touch with Sean, she sure as shit knew that Michael and Sean had not spoken in years, and she was privy to all the details as to why. She saw Michael looking as though he had just run a marathon standing next to Sean, who looked as though he had just seen a ghost. She put this together and made two quick determinations, both of which were horrifying. Either someone was dead, or she was about to receive information that was going to change the remainder of her life.

The doorbell rang. Sean, somewhat terrified to move, explained that it was probably the pizza delivery, and he apologetically slinked out of the room to retrieve it.

Lara locked eyes with her husband, and her eyes started to well with tears. "Pizza, Michael?" She never could have imagined a question so banal would illicit such emotion from her.

"Baby, I need to talk to—"

"Yeah, you think? Listen carefully. I'm going to put Daniel down for a nap, and then you need to have an answer for what I walked in on. No stuttering or stalling or absurd descriptions. I want an answer immediately. Do you understand what I am saying?"

"Yeah."

Michael kissed his son, squeezed him, and placed him down in the direction of his mother. He tapped him on his backside to set him in motion. The look on Lara's face informed him that his story better be complete, or it may be one of the last times he was able to kiss his son in his wife's presence.

As Lara left the room, Sean was returning with several pizza boxes and a young gentleman that he had never seen in his life, but he could not have been dressed any better. Michael could not have imagined this day becoming any more of a fucking caricature than it already had, and now he was faced with the best-looking pizza delivery guy he had ever seen.

"Mike, this is Donald Tressell, a good friend. We met at a church group."

Michael walked around the table to shake Donald's hand. He could not think of a single reason why Donald Tressell would be in his house at this time. His situation seemed to call for a little more than church group friends and prayers. If Donald could perhaps perform an exorcism, that might make him the most useful person in the zip code.

"Donald, I really don't mean to be rude, but I have had an incredibly exhausting day and I didn't think I was going to be entertaining company. Why the fuck are you here?"

"Mike! Can you be a human being for five minutes?"

Donald laughed out loud and let go of Michael's hand. "I came for the free pizza."

"He's here to help us with this mysterious delivery from Vera Conroy."

As Sean began to take his first slice of pizza, the doorbell rang again.

"That would be Ms. Conroy. Donald, have some pizza. Your homework is all on the table. Mike, can you get some plates and drinks?"

Michael felt like he was in a Salvador Dalí painting. He heard Sean in the distance, and he turned to find Donald removing his blazer and rolling up his sleeves. He placed a pair of blue metal thin-framed glasses on his narrow face that seemed as if it had been chiseled to meet the needs of a modeling campaign. Donald stood over the dining room table and slowly scanned what was in front of him, often moving papers slightly to arrange them in a format that he must have felt more comfortable with. He removed a black Montblanc pen from the inside of his blazer, and he began writing vigorously on the blank inside of one of the manila folders. In moments, he had filled almost the entirety of the space, and he stopped to stretch his hand. Michael assumed Donald was in his late twenties but no more than early thirties. Michael spent most of his life sizing men up regarding their physicality. Donald was about six foot three, and he could tell that he worked out regularly. He was also a man who spent a good deal on his wardrobe. Lara would be able to deduce almost immediately who his designer was and how much he spent on his clothing. He didn't need Lara's expertise to inform him that Donald made a very healthy living.

Sean reentered with Vera Conroy as Michael also returned with some plates and bottled water. Michael smiled at Vera and went over to give her a full hug with both of his hands full. Seeing Vera calmed him slightly. Given the situation he had no real reason or right to feel this way but Vera had always provided him with a small maternal sense, and her diminutive nature and her sweetness and warmth always made her one of the best parts of being at St. Catherine's.

As Michael was feeling comforted by Vera's presence, Lara walked into the dining room, having changed into full-on workout gear. Her hair was up in a ponytail, and her Anne Taylor work clothes and heels had been replaced with Lululemon yoga pants, a New York Rangers T-shirt, and a pair of black Nike Air Force 1s. Michael, even in his distressed state, loved this look. He was always convinced that yoga pants were invented solely for his wife, and he was very grateful they existed. She paused to take in all of the new arrivals, and she looked at the pizza delivery as if it had been done solely to irritate her.

Sean placed both of his arms in the air and took a deep breath. He made all the introductions of everyone in the room from that posture and explained the entirety of the day. He looked at everyone and provided a most succinct explanation of the day. He included Stanley Antoine, Ralph DiNardi, mysterious phone calls, and the reunion of two brothers in the back of Ponce's Deli earlier in the day. Michael did not think the events of this nightmarish Tuesday could have been more carefully illustrated by the folks at SparkNotes. Halfway through his monologue, Lara explained her need to sit down. Vera pushed an empty chair in her direction because Michael was too ashamed to approach her. The woman Michael had fallen in love with when they were teenagers appeared ready to break his jaw if he got any closer. She certainly was dressed to go a few rounds. Sean explained that this appeared to be a situation that was much larger than all of them, which Vera confirmed with a vigorous nodding of her head. He ended by notifying everyone there that they had a job to get done and it would begin with Vera providing a brief understanding about her charitable delivery. He also informed the now team that they were to expect a call from someone at the school regarding Michael's absolute "dumbassery." To this point, Lara met Michael's gaze and offered a mocking, spiteful half smile and nod of assurance similar to Vera Conroy's earlier one.

Lara stood up and walked toward the kitchen. "Would anyone care for some wine? I would love some red with my pizza." Her voice was shaky but still managed to convey a hint of sarcasm and exasperation at what her evening and perhaps her life was turning into. "Michael, could you please help me in the kitchen with the bottle?"

This was the specific moment that Michael had feared since his fist connected with Stanley's on a morning that now felt like ten years ago. He was certainly afraid of facing the retribution he deserved for this action and all the violent actions contained in his past. He was even afraid at what this would do to his relationship with his brother. He could not believe that Sean was even speaking to him, let alone acting as his chief of staff in the dining room. The feeling that had grown and matured in Michael's chest throughout the day was shame. For the first time in his life, Michael did not feel justification for his violence. He did not feel righteousness. He did not feel skewed toward his own correctness. He felt shame, and he saw shame in the woman who had just walked into the kitchen awaiting his assistance in opening a fictitious bottle of wine. It was this specific conversation that he was terrified of.

CHAPTER 35

By the time Michael had entered the kitchen, Lara was sitting at the small table with her head being cradled by both of her hands. Her right leg was shaking, and it appeared she was attempting to calm herself by breathing slowly. Michael was well aware of the leg shaking and what it meant. Lara had developed the habit in childhood, and it acted as a companion as she grew into adulthood. It had been visible that day in the stands at the baseball game, it had been highly apparent during the three times Lara took her SATs, and she often had to consciously restrain her leg during high leverage meetings, especially with clients she truly desired to work with.

"Lara...I—"

"Don't you dare."

Michael stopped and attempted to sit down without making any kind of sound that would disturb any item in the universe.

"Do. Not. Sit."

A man that had been involved in some of the most grue-some displays of violence with men twice his size had been shut down by a woman who was refusing to look at him after having said only six words. He slowly and just as quietly pushed the chair back under the table. Lara spoke slowly so as to be as clear as she could. It was also the only way she would be able to speak through the pure emotion she was feeling and the tightness in her chest.

"For years, I experienced a countless number of people who told me and at times even begged me to stay away from you. I stopped counting how many. It would, at times, make me sad for us and, at other times, make me angry with them. Who were these people to tell me anything about the person I loved, and what did they know about us anyway? They would say you were going to end up in jail or you would hurt me one day. They said you couldn't be trusted with this rage that you had located inside of you. They said that you would break my heart and hurt me in ways I could not imagine."

Lara pointed directly at Michael's hands. Her eyes were swollen.

"I saw all the times you came home with cuts and scrapes and bruises. I was always afraid to ask you questions or say something. I wasn't afraid you would ever hurt me or get mad at me for asking. I was always afraid that if I asked, you would actually give me an honest answer and it would end with you having killed someone. So, I never did. I just pretended I didn't notice, and you pretended that nothing happened, and we pre-tended together that you were normal. I always defended you. So did your mom. But we were wrong. We were wrong. We made all of this possible, and we let you think that what you were doing, what this was, was okay. And you and I made a child together, and all those people who warned me, pleaded with me, including Sean, were absolutely right, and you made my defense of you wrong."

Lara pointed directly at Michael and her throat tightened.

"You did that. You could have made them wrong, but instead you chose to make the only two women who really loved you wrong. The years of not really knowing what you were capable of or what would happen next. The years of having knots in my stomach when you were out or when you would call. And to come home to this. You hurt a child. I don't care how big he was or what he had on his phone or that you have always wanted to defend your brother. He's a kid. What his family must think of you, of us? And for what? Sean was the brunt of his cruelty, and he would not have done this! But for some reason, my husband, Daniel's dad, did, and now we have to clean up another car crash. I love you, Michael, and I really dislike myself for it because you've made me just as guilty as you and I never laid a hand on anyone."

It would have been easier if she had been screaming. It would have helped if she had thrown things. It would have helped if she slapped him. She didn't. She sat there without looking at him. She was looking away from him, down to the corner near the floor as if all of what she spoke were written on the wall for her to read. It was clear and tempered with a quiet disposition loud enough for him but not for those in the dining room to hear. She spoke it with next to no physical gestures and almost no emphasis on her face. She looked empty, deflated.

"What can I—"

"You can finish this little 'dinner party' in our dining room, and when everyone leaves, if everyone leaves, you can sleep in the guest room until we figure out what comes next. I would like to make it known now that it won't include me, though."

With her last sentence, Lara looked up at Michael as if to confirm she was finished with him. Michael could see that she had tears beginning to gather in her eyes. Her tightened jaw was working overtime to not let Michael have them, and her folded arms let him know he was dismissed. He felt a tightness in his throat and a sharp pain in his head. He never believed that he would arrive at the day when little Lara Trammell, the tomboy on the swings, didn't want him anymore. Michael's shame was still present, but it was now accompanied by two friends, pure sadness and regret.

It's not easy to leave a room when you don't know exactly how. You know how you got in and you know where the door is, but you don't quite know how to depart. He didn't want to leave. He wanted to stay and beg his wife for another chance. He wanted to get on his knees and swear to God above that this was the last time he would ever put them through something like this. He wanted to negotiate, mediate, and plead with her. But a small part of him knew that those promises might not be kept, even for her and their child. He chose not to lie or beg. He had lied enough for three lifetimes, and Lara's demeanor made it resoundingly clear that she would not be swayed nor persuaded by his promises. Michael chose to simply turn and feel the tightness in his throat increase as he pushed through the swinging wooden door into the dining room. It was evident that beyond that door would be a different life, a different life that did not include his best friend. The only connection between them would be their son.

The cell phone in his pocket had begun ringing while he was standing in front of Lara, and it was at about seven rings when he pulled it from his pocket.

"Hello."

"Well, look at who decided to charge his phone and actually answer it."

His voice was not familiar. It was tinged with sarcasm, and it was abrasive in nature. It took a single sentence for Michael to know he didn't like this person.

"May I help—"

"Oh, you absolutely may help me, Mr. Cloughey. You and I need to have a chat about English class this morning."

"Who is this? Who am I speaking to right now?"

"Don't you worry yourself about that. We will meet soon enough. I am going to text you an address, and you will arrive there. I will happen to have a cell phone that has less than flattering pictures of your brother on it. You will be there in less than one hour."

With that, the call was ended, and Michael looked at Sean with a mixture of confusion and frustration.

"That was the call we were waiting for, Michael, and after what we have been working on in here, it appears as though St. Catherine's is into a little bit more than math and English and college acceptances."

CHAPTER 36

Robert put the phone down, looked at Anya, and then closed both of his eyes. He took a long deep breath in through his nose with both of his hands flat on the desk he now quite despised. He lifted his chin upward as if the air only a few inches above his head were of better quality and let the entire breath out slowly through his lips, which were now in a circular ring. It did not achieve the desired state of inner calm he was searching for.

"*Fuuuuuucccckkkkk!*"

Robert elongated the singular word to the point of turning his face bright red and until his lungs and throat could no longer create sound. Anya jumped and took two steps backward. She had been privy to Robert's anger before, but this was understandably different.

Robert sat back in his chair, palms still flat on the desk, and looked more through Anya than at her. "That's better."

He stood, buttoned the top button of his white dress shirt—now inappropriately wrinkled according to his standards—and he began repairing the quality of the Windsor knot of his tie. Unrolling his sleeves, he walked to the standing mirror in the corner and looked at himself with disgust. He held out both arms as if to suggest nothing could repair his current state of disarray and with the effect of wondering if anything could be worse than what was looking back at him. He shook his head and mumbled something under his breath twice, and Anya swore it was the word "motherfucker." She could not attest to it, however. She was desperately wanting to leave the room.

"Anya, in ten minutes, would you please be so kind as to text the information on my desk to our dear friend Mr. Cloughey? Nothing else, just that. Then please consider your work done for the day, or, should I now say, evening. Thank you for all of your assistance today."

With those words, Robert Hanover walked to his desk and picked up Stanley Antoine's phone and his long coat. He didn't look at Anya again before leaving, but he did stop with his back to her and his hand on the doorknob.

"Ten minutes."

There was no familiar coding to his language, no charisma to his direction or request. He was to the point, as if extra wording or terminology was too exhausting to conjure. As he pulled the door closed behind him, Anya waited a few seconds until she could hear the heavy outer door of their office record its familiar thud as it closed. She exhaled as it felt like she had been holding her breath since Hanover's outburst. Walking over to the desk, she spotted a single piece of lined paper. It was torn almost in half on a bit of a jagged slant, and the writing in black ink resembled more a hostage letter than a note. Turning it upright, she squinted to make out the handwriting.

"Is this even an address?"

CHAPTER 37

By the time Michael had hung up from his slightly mysterious and even further annoying phone call, he was met with Lara crossing past him in a blur to return to the chair she had vacated earlier. She had promised herself internally that she would leave the kitchen and abscond to the bedroom until the band of misfit toys had left her home. A part of her, a small part of her, was highly interested in what the second half of a day looked like after your husband beat up a boy and managed to stay out of handcuffs. Funny thing about patience is that you don't truly know exactly how much you have until you are forced to exercise it on every level. Aside from Lara, the team assembled forces, and both Donald Tressell and Vera Conroy were setting up the dining room table to resemble what looked like a makeshift corkboard where serial killers are tracked in one-hour television dramas. However, she was convinced that this would last longer than one hour, and it was in no way entertaining. Lastly, Sean appeared to be working up a narration for all of this so that it would make some sort of sense. Michael explained that time was not on their side as he had a little under ten minutes until he received further instructions from the mystery man. Lara's crossed-arm, straight-backed body language read as though he would have had just short of that in her hands if this group had left.

Sean began with somewhat of a smile on his face but also a serious intention attached to his demeanor, the proverbial cat-that-caught-the-canary look.

"What it appears is that St. Catherine's was acting as a very elaborate and incredibly well administered front for some very heavy-duty money laundering."

Michael, unable to sit due to his growing anxiety, placed both hands on his knees to either alleviate the anxiety or to try to brace himself. "What?! Are you serious about this?"

"We are 100 percent serious about this, and we have all of the information here to prove it and shine an enormous fucking spotlight on this. No one in this room is excusing, forgiving, or even condoning what you did to your student this morning. If it were up us, you would already be getting processed and arraigned."

Lara perked up at the idea of Sean's last sentence to chime in with a reassuring and confirming "Ahem."

"So, my dear brother, I asked myself all day since I heard of your exploits, why, in fact, have you not been arrested? Why were the police never called? Why do you exist here in front of us right now without having had to answer to the family?"

Vera chimed in by raising her hand meekly in the back of the room as if she was afraid to disturb the proceedings.

"Early in the afternoon a few reporters did call Mr. DiNardi, and he was incredibly—how shall I put it—well, visibly perturbed. He told me to just take messages, and he closed his door halfway to make a phone call. His call was at a half whisper, but I know he was speaking with Mr. Hanover."

"The chairman of the board of St. Catherine's?"

"Oh yes, Mr. Cloughey, him. Have you ever met him? He is quite a piece of work. Very to the point and a bit too straight-forward. A little sarcastic for my liking."

"Not in person, but I do have a very strong feeling that I just spoke with him on the phone right now. We are meeting, and he wants to discuss my actions and give me Stanley's phone. Why would he want to give me Stanley's phone?"

Sean replied promptly to this item.

"Well, if he's the board chair, Mike, he probably wants all of this to get put to bed, right? He doesn't want police or the media to ask questions or get too involved in what is really going on at the school."

Lara, fully engaged now, stood up and raised her hand.

"Okay, can we just agree that, since I will never be a teacher again, this dining room does not have to resemble my English class? If you've got something, spit it out. No need for hands."

Lara looked at her husband and kept her hand raised until she was recognized by Sean.

"Vera, does anyone know that this material was in your hands or even missing at all?"

"Oh, no, no, no, Mrs. Cloughey. I retrieved all of this from the second in command in the finance department at the school. A Mr. Kevin Webster came to the school about five years ago to revamp all the IT systems that are used to handle finances. Mr. DiNardi told me to give him, how do you call it, carte blanche?" Vera tried her best French pronunciation of the term. "He said he came from 'on high,' a little joke Mr. DiNardi would make when he would refer to the board. Well, it just so happens that I was asked to create a password for Mr. DiNardi as access to this stuff is kept pretty tight. So I did create that password, and I gave it to Mr. Webster. Since Mr. DiNardi liked the password, he never changed it. It's ROLEX. I named it after a horse his wife owns. All I needed to do was go into his email, retrieve the link, use his email and password, and I got it."

Donald, sensing it was time for him to finally put some professional polish to the conversation, decided he would stand. Without the hand raise, he began with explaining that most accounts such as this require a two-factor authorization where they send a code, and you can only gain access to the account after it has been applied.

"Oh no, they never did that, Mr. Tressell. Just the email and good old Rolex."

Vera placed her hand over her mouth and tittered as if she had pulled a fast one over everybody at the school and was equivalent to some sort of a black hat hacker.

Sean took a moment to express his deep and profound love for Vera Conroy and then stepped to the side to let Donald continue his explanation.

"All right, I will try to make this brief because you are expecting a text in about two minutes and forty-nine seconds. From what these files display, it appears that individuals are claiming that there are almost four thousand students enrolled at your school. Vera confirms that there are, in fact, only a little over one thousand and two hundred students enrolled. That means we have an accounting system set up for approximately two thousand and eight hundred extra students. Names like Isabelle Ryberg, Dexter Davidson, Ryan Southerland, and Patrice Lacavelli have never been students at the school. Yet these imaginary students have been paying the maximum tuition, fees, and book payments for years. Just say you take twenty-eight hundred kids and multiply it by thirty-five thousand dollars in tuition. You arrive at approximately—"

Lara's leg stopped twitching, and she immediately blurted out, "Approximately ninety-eight million dollars."

Donald slapped the table, pointed at her, and said, "Ninety-eight million dollars. The lady wins the teddy bear." He concluded with a brief smile.

On a normal day, this little exchange between Lara and Donald would have made Michael wildly jealous. It felt unnecessary and somewhat flirtatious, and Lara seemed to enjoy the attention of Donald a bit too much at that moment. However, this was not the time nor place to address this, and Michael could blame Lara for nothing at this point. He was the cause of this pain and the reason Donald was there constructing a financial autopsy that painted his current employers as thieves on a grand scale. Lara was a beautiful woman. She was sophisticated, smart, funny, and always pleasant. She could befriend an ice cube faster than it could melt on an afternoon in August. Michael felt threatened by her beauty, but his jealousy was always brief as Lara always dismissed even the most obvious flirting. She was the most dedicated friend and partner there was, and Michael knew she was desired. Lara would laugh at him and mock him as she said, "Oh, poor Michael. He has a pretty wife. Poor guy. Must be terrible for him." They would normally end with their typical, humorous prodding. It was not as if Michael was not flirted with. Lara always mentioned something a woman did that was a flirtatious act. Michael was incredibly aloof in this regard, and he would often tell her she was crazy. Lara, in a cocky way, would always tell him that she liked it that other women wanted her husband. It not only reinforced her taste but also her decision to marry her maniac.

"But how the fuck do you get away with something like this? No checks and balances? Audits? How?"

"It appears that the company that provides the yearly audit is listed as an Edinburgh Global."

"Wouldn't this firm know that this is all bullshit and that the school is scamming people?"

"They most certainly would, and they would be red-flagging it and performing their due diligence to get in there and figure out how a magical ninety-eight mill just shows up. Only problem is…"

Donald spun his laptop around so that it faced Sean from across the table. It was open to Edinburgh Global's web page masthead. With a wry smile, Donald stated,

"Mr. Robert Hanover is listed as the CEO of Edinburgh Global."

Donald added, "And the audit reads spotless from what I can gather here. Robert Hanover happens to be an incredibly large player in hedge funds, especially quants."

Michael rubbed the sticky sweat from his forehead, "Fuck me. Absolutely fuck me sideways."

With that piece of information, even the portion that most of the room had no idea of the language being spoken or the proper understanding of what it all meant, there was a collective combination of a gasp and a sigh. It was as if everyone in the room were watching the same movie with the same surprise ending. It also signified the end of the "creative accounting tutorial" that Donald Tressell was providing. Michael felt his phone vibrate, signifying the much-anticipated text: *Angilotti's. Back entrance. 30 mins. Alone.*

CHAPTER 38

THE NOW BETTER-EDUCATED CAST OF THE DINING room was still partly reeling from the shock of the intensity of the news they just received mixed with the troubling news that Michael was being summoned alone. This most unofficial invitation changed the entire demeanor of the meeting to, as Lara described it, "creepy as fuck." Those present agreed with her assessment and that the day was now even more perverse in nature. What had started out as a gross and despicable action on the part of Michael Cloughey seemed to be ending with a powerful man attempting to threaten him in a way that sent a profound message.

Michael, having seen the picture of Robert Hanover and half listening to the murmurings in the room, began getting dressed and prepared to leave.

"Michael, what are you doing?"

"What do you mean, Sean?"

"How are you considering this absurd meeting?"

"C'mon, look at the guy. I can get the phone and see what the fuck he wants. He's a fucking pencil pusher. He probably works out and does Pilates with a trainer at his gym. You're taking this as a threat? He probably just wants nobody to see him. He wants to hide and do this under the cover of night. I will be back in no time, and I can finally get some sleep. It's late."

Lara interjected, "I think you're being way too glib about this. You don't know this guy or what he's capable of. For once in your life, stop and ask yourself why the events of this day have played out the way they have. We just got a pretty nice education as to what this school is, and what *he* is about. You think he's some weak guy with a tie, but he has ninety-eight million reasons to want to shut you up."

Michael was surprised that Lara still had the ability to use an affectionate term regarding him. For a second, he allowed that gesture to give him a breath of hope that his wife might still love him. It was all he had. One word. He placed his hands on both of her shoulders and looked into her eyes. He wanted to relax her, but he was also trying desperately to make a brief connection with her.

"Lara, believe me, I understand all of the concerns here, and I am very thankful, but if he is going to do anything, he is probably going to bribe me to go away and never talk about this."

Vera stated, somewhat proud of herself, "Well, Mr. Cloughey, he shouldn't actually have any idea that I brought all of this here. He isn't aware that you even know any of this."

"Well, then I have the upper hand here. If he gets crazy, I can just shut him down with all this, and then I walk away and let them know that I will get out of their hair."

Vera contributing gave Donald a bit more confidence to offer up some words of caution. It gave the appearance that Donald had seen some things in his experience but was confining his advice to this particular episode. "Actually, Michael, I don't know if mentioning any of this is a good idea at all. I think you get the phone and apologize repeatedly and see what he wants and get out of there as quickly as possible. We just discovered that this guy has been using a well-established academic institution as a shell for God-knows-what kind of activity. He definitely is not alone in keeping this all a very well-hidden secret. We also don't know who he is cleaning this money for. Who does he know? Who are his business partners? This could all go really deep."

"Donald, look, I know we just met, and I have a great deal of respect for what you literally brought to the table tonight on my behalf. I respect all of you tremendously and love you all. You didn't have to do any of this. But I'm very thankful. I also know that if Robert Hanover is looking for a bit of a fight, then my brother and wife can assure you that I am usually pretty happy to bring the chips and dips to that. He doesn't look like much, honestly."

"Mike, at least let me come with you. I can just be off in the distance. I don't care. This is just suspicious, and the whole day has smelled off. You weren't arrested or punished, they let you go home, they haven't called to arrange a parent meeting, and you haven't even been issued an official reprimand. Please stop and think here."

"Okay, look, I am finalizing this right now. Sean, I would not take you to this meeting because if this guy does want to get nasty, with all respect, I would not want or need you there. I'm sorry. You're not a fighter. I started this shitty day early this morning, and I want to own what I have done and move on. I am tired and really need this to end."

Lara sighed and started cleaning up and mumbled the word "thickheaded" under her breath loud enough for Michael to hear. Vera, visibly nervous due to the most recent portion of the conversation, began to help while Sean and Donald stood there almost frozen by inactivity and disbelief.

Michael finished getting dressed, and his demeanor shifted. Sean knew this demeanor, and he never liked it. He had seen it before and the aftereffects of it his entire life, and he remembered what it felt like to be on the receiving end of this side of his brother. The conversation just seemed to get him even a little more charged up, and it created inside of him a combination of fear and sadness. He never knew what his brother was capable of doing, but he felt compelled to remind him of one specific thing.

"Mikey, I know you're pissed off, and I get it, but listen to me for one second, please. Look at me."

Both Vera and Lara were in the kitchen, and Donald was organizing all the materials that had been used throughout the evening.

Sean ushered Michael into the living room, hoping the scenery shift of about ten feet would change his brother's point of view.

Michael sighed and looked at his brother. He was still perturbed but he walked with him.

"Please remember that whatever this guy says or shows you, it's nonsense. It truly doesn't matter. Do not hurt anyone else. Please, let it just…go. You are a dad, and the little boy upstairs is going to want to play catch and grow up with his father present. Please hear me."

Michael swallowed hard. Somewhere in his message, Sean captured their entire relationship up to that moment. Who could imagine that even a few days ago that they would be talking to each other at all, and there they were breaking down and sharing time, discovering all the sordid shit that was behind St. Catherine's? If Yah could have seen them now, she would have smiled and hugged them both while their dad sighed at how their mother coddled them. This touched Michael in a place he hated to visit emotionally. There was so much he and Sean needed to speak about, move past, and look forward to, and this day and night felt like an amazing start to reclaim their brotherhood. If he could manage to stay out of jail, this could be a reality for him, and his little boy could grow up with his Uncle Sean. He knew he would need to spend an inordinate amount of time repairing his marriage and getting Lara to get past this day and regain her trust in him as a human being. He knew this would be the biggest challenge, and it scared him to a point where he wanted to vomit.

"Sean, I've never told you this. I've said it to myself a million times. I couldn't have been any luckier to have you as my brother. I've hurt you in ways I can't even imagine, and the years we didn't speak were even worse than I could have imagined. I did all of this, and you were here. You were here with me to help me and support me and love me, and I have no right to have someone like you as my brother. And yet here you are. I love you, and if you even questioned that for a minute in your life, then I am so sorry."

With those words, Michael put on his coat and hat and gloves. Before he left, he yelled out, "Love you, babe. Be back soon." A part of him wasn't able to physically see her face. It was too painful in the moment. He would not allow himself that tenderness at that point. There seemed no way to use that feeling for this meeting. Seeing her always meant so much. He ran upstairs to give the baby a quick kiss, and then he came down and opened a drawer in a small mahogany credenza near the entryway door to retrieve a pair of brass knuckles. He slid them in his pocket and then turned to leave.

CHAPTER 39

Teresa Angilotti had a discernible duality to her personality, and it translated into how she ran her business. Her coffee shop was a very popular feature of the St. Catherine's campus. It was heavily occupied by students, faculty, and staff from morning opening at six to full close at five in the evening. Students would use the tables to sidle up and attempt to share their homework while enjoying the student specials. Faculty would usually make pit stops to pick up a quick bite or indulge in one of the store's coffee specialties. Teresa worked to produce her own coffee blend, and it almost immediately became a crowd favorite. An Ethiopian and Kona blend that she branded "Sunrise Roast" became a secret key component of her varied baked goods such as tiramisu, almond croissants, and her cinnamon muffins. Teresa had inherited the space from family and put a lot of money back into the place in the form of decor, furniture, and antiques. The wall shelves displayed old-fashioned coffee presses, grinders, and varied espresso sets, and she even hired a muralist to pay homage to St. Catherine's Prep by commissioning a mural on the avenue side of the store. There were places in some neighborhoods that seem to fight where they were. They seemed resistant to embrace what was around them, and it felt almost uncomfortable for longtime residents of a neighborhood to even enter. It was as if stopping by was an act equivalent to being a traitor. But Angilotti's always felt like you were in the right place and getting a cup of coffee and seeing Teresa felt like a hug at any time of the day. Teresa, being one of the most relaxed individuals who ever graced the planet, gave up her shop as a gift to the neighborhood, its residents, and in particular the numerous students of St. Catherine's. She was all in on fundraisers, donations, and discounts. Teresa even hosted faculty meetings, staying open a little later to get the teachers fed while they sat through the tedium of administrative policy and a litany of ideas that the board of trustees would never even give any consideration. In return for all her love and loyalty, the entire community embraced Angilotti's as their home away from home. Except in this case, this home away from home came fully stocked daily with freshly made madeleines.

When a store like Angilotti's makes itself what it is to a community, the community in return protects it with every fiber of its pavement and patronage. No one would dare to even so much as litter outside of the store or carve an absurd declaration of love into one of the tables. To do so was mutiny, and it was met with a quick corrective reprimand. At least that's the way it should be and the way Teresa hoped the mutual transaction would occur.

Around the time that Teresa began redecorating and adding her poignant and well-placed antiques, several teachers and some neighborhood residents suggested that she outfit the entire establishment with the full gamut of closed-circuit camera equipment. The estimates for all of this came to a few thousand to install the tech and have it connected to her home computer and cell phone. Teresa smiled, folded up the estimate, and placed it in the bottom section of the drawer underneath the cash register. It was her special place to hold all items that she would think of from time to time but never really give much true attention to. She was a throwback in a time where everything and everyone could be tracked. Michael had even compared Angilotti's to his students as the opposite of what Orwell was trying to arrive at in his novel *1984*: "Big Brother did not reside at Angilotti's." His junior honor students would always chuckle at this joke.

Teresa never honestly thought that there would come a day, as much as she loved her beautiful shop, that she would feel the need to drill security cameras into her building. She was right, and the worst that would ever happen was the occasional teenage make-out session behind the dumpster or the brief marijuana purchase. Aside from those gross travesties of justice, the phrase "Meet you at Angilotti's" took on a host of meanings, mostly reminiscent of happiness.

The directive of Robert Hanover in his text calmed Michael. Nothing bad ever happened at Angilotti's, and Michael had made hundreds of stops there for coffee and dessert. He would often surprise Lara with her favorite, a chocolate cannoli, on Fridays after work. The meeting place just instilled in him a sense of a quick fix, and while he was nervous about meeting Robert Hanover, his normally accurate gut told him he would be home in time to put the baby to bed. He may even get the opportunity to start the massive renovation that would be needed to repair his relationship.

It had gotten colder outside since he arrived home ear-lier and prior to the curtain being pulled wide open on St. Catherine's Prep. It was windy, and the cold seemed to bite at his exposed face. As he walked, he decided to say as little as possible at this little get-together and to be incredibly sto-ic in his response and demeanor. He just wanted the phone and to offer up an apology for the mess he created. He had no idea how Robert Hanover would receive him or his apology. Making a man as wealthy as Hanover leave what was probably a lavish home or penthouse in this cold was not something that inspired patience or the most understanding of sentiments. He wondered if he didn't have some sort of assistant or lackey who did this kind of stuff on his behalf. He even wondered if DiNardi would be there to stand by with his familiar dopey grin and his self-aggrandizing demeanor. Michael had a lot of questions rolling through his head, and his energy level grew with each cold block. The cold, as much as he disliked it, did recharge the lungs and nose, and the quick pace of his walk caused him to sweat slightly under his clothing. He wondered for a moment, *If it is this cold just before Thanksgiving, what does the rest of the winter have in store?*

The cold and impending snow always calmed things down. They kept people in, kept cars off the road, and they created a sleepy sense to even the busiest of neighborhoods. As Michael hit Windsor Place, he could see Angilotti's in the distance. The lights were off. It was still too early for the bakers to arrive and perform their evening magic. He was in the mood for a hot cof-fee. Michael saw a car in the distance with its lights on. It looked like a four-door model luxury car, but he couldn't confirm.

Hanover sat inside his car, scrolling through his phone. His sense of impatience was at the highest point he could possibly imagine. His driver tried to engage in small talk, and all he did was respond with "Mmm." It was his polite way of saying, "Can you just shut up and face forward?" He placed both of his hands on his face as if to wipe something from it, and he followed that with a deep and heavy sigh. As he was at the finality of his exhale, his phone buzzed: *I'm here.*

"Well, Mr. Cloughey appears to be a man of few words. Okay. Time to go."

CHAPTER 40

"Mr. Hanover?"

"That is I and I am him. Mr. Cloughey, I really should be at home right now."

Robert was informed of how small Michael Cloughey was, but it wasn't until he was standing next to him looking down slightly that he got an actual sense of the man.

"Yeah, please allow me to offer up my—"

"Please save it, Michael. I'm already here, you're already here, and it seems we have a fine reservation here by this wonderful dumpster in the cold. We're a little bit beyond apologies."

"So then may I ask what we are doing here tonight? It also seems, by the fact that your incredibly expensive car is still running, that I came alone but you did not."

Robert ignored the second half of Michael's statement and focused on the actual question. He had decided quite some time ago that this meeting would occur only according to his terms, requests, and directives.

"Well, sure you may. For some time now, you and Mr. Antoine have had a bit of a contentious relationship. It's as if you are standing on some sort of moral high ground regarding his grades and attendance, and this is causing him and his family quite a bit of strife. They are a hardworking family, having pulled themselves up by their proverbial bootstraps, and they want nothing more than to see their son and their incredibly bright daughter succeed. Stanley, agreeably, is not a scientist, but what he is missing in the IQ department, he certainly makes up for when he got on line twice for physicality."

"Yeah, he's a pretty talented—"

"Yes. He is a pretty talented athlete, and you took it upon yourself to cave his jaw in this morning. And why did you do this? Why?"

"Look, Mr. Hanover, I am incredibly ashamed of what I did, and I couldn't be any sorrier for my actions."

Robert Hanover reintroduced the tone from his opening sentence. It was acerbic with an attempt at wit, but it also held the posture of his loathsome feelings toward Michael and this entire experience. The fact that Michael was attempting to apologize made his tongue sharper, and with each of Michael's attempts to interject, Hanover grew more biting. He had challenged corporate giants, stout men of stature, men who challenged his reserve, his intellect, and his financial bottom line. Michael Cloughey, his stature, and his apologetic demeanor felt weak and insulting to his attendance in this alleyway. This teacher punched a student unconscious this morning, a young man who eclipsed him in size, and here he was now, standing and shivering in the cold and feeling remorseful. Robert was as much annoyed by Michael's lack of conviction as he was having to be present. Above all things Robert hated was a lack of true conviction in all actions. You can't behave one way in the morning and then be sorrowful late that night. Own your actions, embrace what and who you are, and apologize to no one for getting the job done. That is, in fact, what it was all about. These were some of the reinforcing beliefs that Robert used in his business, and the tone he was being introduced to at this moment worked in opposition to his pedigree.

"Oh, okay. Well, I guess that just does it. Problem solved. Let's all go home and get all warmed up. This morning you had a teenager play a class A trick on you after riding you for months, and you couldn't handle it. I mean, what are you, a twelve-year-old who can't handle getting teased by a kid?"

"No, it goes beyond that, actually."

"Does it? You know, I've seen what's on the phone. The kid photoshops some pictures of your priest brother sucking some dick and taking it in the ass, and you have a nervous breakdown. I did a little research on you, and you have had quite a healthy history of being a violent little man. It appears that this just seems to be how you handle shit in your life. Perhaps we can also point to the more than obvious fact that you are a white male who felt the need to impose some sort of physical superiority over a young student from a minority group. We haven't even touched upon that aspect of this. But if you push me, I will make this out to be that in every way, shape, and form."

"Now just wait. It truly is more than how you are painting it right now, and I don't appreciate the reference to my brother in that fashion. This also has nothing to do with Stanley's ethnicity. I would like to have a conversation and obtain the phone from you and just get out of the way of you and Ralph and St. Catherine's."

"Yes. A bit of research informed me quite nicely about you. You once almost beat another young man your age to the point of being a cripple because he apparently beat you in a baseball game? Wow. And there was another student who was beaten in the bathroom of the school a while ago, a young man who had issues. Now, no one has confirmed this gem, but I am willing to place a slight wager that it was you. But even if we let that go, we still have other instances of you living a life that both Virginia and John could not be incredibly proud of."

The last sentence locked Michael Cloughey in. He had done all he could to avoid eye contact with this man, partly out of shame for his actions and partly out of dislike for this person from what he had just learned a short time ago in his warm dining room. However, hearing the first name of both of his parents in this exchange changed his posture. He immediately made deep eye contact with Robert Hanover and started to feel his shoulder blades and stomach tighten. The sweat that had formed on his frame earlier was back, but now it was incredibly warm. He could feel his heart rate intensify. His palms were wet as he let out a breath. He hoped the breath would assist him in remembering his promise to behave.

"All right, I want to be done here, Mr. Hanover. So let's not be in the habit of mentioning any more of my family or friends or my life. I believe you have a phone for me, and that's why we are here."

Hanover took one step toward Michael and returned his eye contact. "Oh, you are quite right. I did have a phone for you. I was even going to make you an offer tonight. I was going to give you the phone, a sizable check, and a light wave good-bye with the instructions to go get your wife and your kid and your brother and go the fuck away forever. From what I have gathered, I am pretty confident the entire design community wouldn't miss Lara that much anyway."

Michael's hands left his pockets and immediately arrived at the coat collar of Robert Hanover. Everything turned to a shadow for a second as he twisted the jacket tight around the lower neck of this man. He took a sharp step forward with his right foot, and he twisted his grip to force Hanover off-balance and down to the ground. Hanover's back landed flatly against the dumpster. It was where Michael wanted to place him. Robert let out a deep, pained groan from the immediate impact.

"I don't want your fucking money. Give me the fucking phone and leave me the fuck alone."

Michael placed both hands on the top of the dumpster and used the leverage to press his boot into Hanover's waist right below the rib cage. Hanover, visibly rocked by the moment and his immediate position, raised both of his arms up as he tried to gather his breath and thoughts.

"Fuck, now I see it. There you are. Jesus Christ. Okay. Okay."

Michael removed his foot from Hanover's waist and stepped back, breathing deeply. His shoulders were hunched forward, and he widened his stance in case Hanover was in the mood to challenge him. He didn't get a sense that Hanover was the kind of person who had exchanges like this very often in his life. It was not a business that many people wished to entertain. To be this and to do this meant that you were okay with taking something physically from someone while also being okay with them taking something from you in return. That exchange was a transaction of fear, of pain, of sadness. Michael felt two of those three things at that moment.

"I am getting up. Just stop it. Take a breath."

Hanover stood and raised his hands again as if to surrender this moment. His head and posture dropped slightly. He lightly began to brush off the back of his coat. Looking down, he saw the caked dirt outline of Michael's boot by his midsection. He was out of breath and sweating. He placed his hand on the back of his head to confirm that his landing against the dumpster had not cracked a portion of his head open.

"I am calling my driver to bring the phone. Just wait one second."

Michael took another step back. He caught his breath and returned his hands to his pockets. He was disappointed in his inability to secure the phone and get home without this happening. His desire to be home at this moment in the arms of his wife was immeasurable. It was the safest place he knew and the only place he had ever wanted to be since he was a teenager.

"Alex, please bring me the phone. Also, please text Anya and let her know we are a wrap here."

Those words calmed Michael slightly. He was still feeling his elevated heart rate, but hearing Hanover say those words did make him feel an exit to this nightmare. Hanover ended his call and placed his phone back in his pocket delicately. He looked at Michael with an expression as if to say, "Truce."

"Perhaps I underestimated you and your Citizen watch and your Timberland boots. You may have ruined a coat that cost three thousand dollars and a Rolex that cost four times that."

"When exactly do you shut the fuck up? We can wait for Alex with you in the actual dumpster."

"I'm just exchanging some small talk. That's all. Don't go all Hulk again."

Robert Hanover continued speaking, but it was incomprehensible to Michael. He heard no other sound. His ears immediately stopped working. His stomach tightened, and the fingers of his left hand entered the holes of the brass knuckles in his jacket pocket. His jaw clenched so tightly he felt as if he would break several of his teeth. To his left about thirty or so yards away, he saw two of the largest men he had ever viewed in his life. His head turned to take them from his peripheral view to full forward. He felt his phone buzzing in his pocket. He had no time to discern whether this was a call or a text, but he imagined it was Sean checking on him. The shadow of his vision cleared, and he turned to immediately face Hanover. Hanover's head was tilted to the side, and he was wearing a slight half grin that suggested a sense of pride.

"What the fuck is this?"

"*This* is my driver, Alex, and his brother, Louis. They are employees, and they are here to deliver your phone. You're not the only person who has a brother, although there is a slight difference between them and you and the venerable Pastor Cloughey."

"You are a motherfucker, Hanover."

Michael wanted to stop and explain that if these two individuals made a move that he would immediately take all the information he had directly to the police and blow the entire lid off St. Catherine's and all those individuals behind it. He wanted to pick up his phone and make a call. He wanted to immediately attack Robert Hanover and strangle him to death. He did none of those things because he was immediately and intently sizing up Alex and Louis.

Everyone had weaknesses somewhere, and he was immediately trying to find one for each of them. It was going to come to this, and his sense of acceptance was growing rapidly. He couldn't run. They held the entrance, and the wall behind him was too high. There was simply no place for him to go but through them. This being his only option made him perform the math that he would first go after the knee or ankle of one while making every attempt to use the brass knuckles to at least stun the other enough to create enough space for him to gather and run. The equation also informed him that the legs of both Alex and Louis were equivalent to tree trunks, and he would also need to find an angle to put his fist anywhere near the face of the other. He estimated they were about six-four or six-five in height. Their faces also suggested that they were not strangers to being punched, probably by men a lot bigger than him.

"I am going to leave you here to discuss all of this with them. It would also appear that they forgot the phone somewhere back at the office. They are rather forgetful at times. I really try to find capable people, but it is not always easy." To this, Alex gave a slight smirk. "I would love to say this has been a pleasure, but it's been kind of like making out with my sister."

"Hanover, you can just let me go. I won't be a problem."

Robert Hanover buttoned his coat and raised the collar. The snow started to build and blanket everything, pristine snow putting the dirty streets to sleep.

"Goodbye, Michael."

Before he made his exit, Hanover whispered something in the ear of one of the men. He bent and twisted his head around to receive the words, and Michael saw this as an opportunity. He took two giant steps forward to gain some momentum and came down with as much force as he could to slide into the kneecap of the man speaking to Hanover. It was as if he were sliding into second base again, but instead of keeping the lead leg flat, he let it come up right under the knee. His attempt was to chop this man down to a more reasonable size. The other, somewhat stunned by Michael's speed and aggression, almost paused to take this in.

Before Michael could get off the ground, however, he was in an incredibly firm grasp and his bucking did not free him. He returned the grasp with one of his own. As he was thrown into the full side of the dumpster, his attempt was to bring this man down with him. Michael felt himself hit the dumpster and then felt the immediate weight of his attacker land flush on top of him. His head rapped against the edge of the dumpster and sent a spike of pain down his neck and shoulders.

He reached desperately into his jacket and slipped his wet hand into his brass knuckles. Freeing them, he made several connecting punches into the side of the face and head of either Alex or Louis. He simply didn't know who was who at this point, and attendance was not the first area of concern at the moment. Michael could feel his punches landing fully and at one point could feel the metal digging deep into skin. He was convinced he would not stop until he felt bone. As he was rapidly throwing punches, he could see his next problem approaching as the first guy was up and attempting to stabilize himself on his uncertain leg. Michael knew he had only a few seconds, but he was winded and incredibly dizzy. He assumed he was concussed, but he told himself to get home now. He threw one more punch at the back of the head of the man lying on top of him and attempted to lift him off him. He was giving up at least a hundred pounds to each of these guys, and he was feeling it. This needed to end quickly if it was going to end in his favor. As he turned to shove the body weight off him and take one breath, Michael felt a full punch to his face at the top of the cheekbone. The punch was followed by more weight on top of him. Apparently, the damage he did to the knee of what was probably Alex was enough to make standing or walking incredibly difficult.

Everything went black in Michael's world. The snow, the distance, these men—all gone. He was sleepy, and he tasted a thick stream of blood in his mouth. He almost choked when he attempted to swallow, so he spit out what he believed was at least one tooth into the face of man now face-to-face with him. His problem now, however, was he was faced with the weight of two men on top of him. He needed to stand, but with incredibly clouded vision, growing dizziness, and enormous fatigue, it would be like trying to steady a toddler. Michael lurched his face forward in the dark, and he used his mouth to bite deeply into a portion of what he thought was a nose. He felt his teeth sinking into flesh and heard an intense scream. He tasted blood but could not determine if it was his or not. It made no difference as the weight rolled off him. He heard the two men yelling at each other, but he could not decipher what they were communicating. He kept telling himself to stand up, just stand up. Michael got himself to his knees, and he grasped several times for the edge of the dumpster for assistance. Michael's normal self would be disgusted by having his body and face pressed against this garbage receptacle, but now it was providing a life-saving purpose. He knew this was not simply a beating to send a message. This was Hanover's way of erasing his problem. His goodbye was more a farewell than a good night.

Michael got to his feet and felt the entirety of the universe spinning. He vomited and was unable to ground himself. He was shaking, and his legs were taffy. He turned slowly and stumbled slightly against one of the walls of Angilotti's. He took several deep breaths and felt his pocket for his brass knuckles. They were not present. He wiped his face with his coat sleeve and reached down to gather snow to clean his face. He squinted and had vision in the eye that was not damaged. He looked down, and most of the snow in the vicinity was varied shades of red. He could see both men, one standing hunched over with hands on his knees and the other propped up on one knee. His face was covered in blood. Michael saw the alley; he saw the hazy streetlights in the distance, and even using one eye, he saw a clear path to walk forward. Every portion of his body was in agony, and his breath, visible in the cold air, was labored.

He took two steps, and if he could make it a few more, he knew he could make the street to perhaps wave a passing car for assistance. He saw one of the men slowly approaching from his left, he saw his brass knuckles on the ground, and he saw his hands cut open. What he did not see, what he could not see, was Alex. What he could not see was the knife that Alex was holding. What he could not see was the speed at which he was being approached. What Michael felt was a tremendous pressure in his rib cage and a slight popping feeling. This was followed by a feeling of warmth.

He immediately fell to the ground and gasped for air. It was not available. He began to panic and cough and swing his arms feebly while lying flat on his stomach. His third cough produced a stream of blood from his mouth. His ears were ringing. He rolled over and saw both men standing over him. He wanted to be home. He wanted to see Lara. He wanted to be on the couch watching television with her, holding each other tightly. He thought of his son. His brother. His parents. He closed his eyes and thought about just trying to get up. He couldn't. He didn't.

Both men moved quickly. One grabbed the pair of brass knuckles.

"Hanover said to take his phone. Anya's going to wipe it."

Louis reached into Michael's pocket and took his phone and his wallet. It would look like a robbery gone wrong. A robbery gone wrong that resembled a small massacre in an alleyway behind one of the most comforting places you could spend any time at in this relatively quiet, small neighborhood entitled Windsor Terrace. Both men gathered themselves, scanned the entirety of the lot, and walked as quickly as they could manage to the car where Robert Hanover sat in the back on his phone. He looked up.

"Well, that took a bit too long, quite frankly."

"He was a tough little bastard."

"You're both ex-military and the size of a small village. Kind of difficult to feel sympathy for either of you. He was probably about a buck forty with rocks in his pockets."

Louis wiped his face with a rag that slightly resembled the Shroud of Turin. Hanover chuckled slightly and tapped Alex on the shoulder.

"So would you like to sit here longer and wait for assistance, or can we leave now?"

The car shifted quickly, and the wheels spun slightly due to the buildup of snow. It recovered itself, caught the green light at the corner, and made an immediate right turn.

CHAPTER 41

THE NEWS REPORTED THE DEATH OF MICHAEL Cloughey as a result of a robbery in the late evening hours. His body had been discovered by a local man walking his dog at 11:52 p.m. He was led down the alleyway by his dog, who must have caught on the scent of blood under the snow and Michael's exposed body. He frantically called the authorities, who, after a short period of time, matched Michael's likeness to calls received by the 72nd Precinct from a Lara Cloughey. A detective and uniformed officer approached the steps of the Cloughey house the following morning. Through the glass of the front door, Lara could see the uniform, and she fell to her knees and screamed. Sean, who had sat upright on the couch all night, unable to sleep, sprang to an immediate stance. He ran to open the door and pick up Lara. He knew the reason for their visit, and he weakly helped Lara to the couch. He thought he might need help getting himself up as well.

The detective stayed for over two hours with the officer waiting outside. They discussed the entirety of the day before and that Michael was not simply robbed. Detective Thomas Dunham took his notes and asked an incredibly long number of questions. He explained that Michael was not in possession of a phone or a wallet. He explained that he had placed a request for phone records, but according to early results, the last call in or out of Michael's phone was to Sean late in the afternoon. There were no texts after that point as well. Michael's boss, a Ralph DiNardi, reported that Michael had been let go the afternoon prior for insubordination and conduct unbecoming a teacher of St. Catherine's Prep Academy. His office released a statement that, while Mr. Cloughey had been terminated from employment, this was an absolute tragedy and that the entire St. Catherine's community was in mourning over the loss of one of their own. Mr. Cloughey touched the lives of many students at the school, and he would be sorely missed. They also offered their deepest condolences to the family and friends of Mr. Cloughey. Detective Dunham explained that, whatever had gone on, Michael put up a valiant effort. He also told them it appeared as though the cause of death was a stab wound to the lung that caused massive internal bleeding. He could not inform them of more than that at the time. The crime scene was still being actively worked on, and there would be more results from an autopsy. He did explain that because of the snow and sleet they were not expecting much to come from a canvas of the crime scene. He quietly and respectfully requested that Lara perform an identification for their official records.

Lara said nothing. She sat with both hands on her knees, feeling nothing. She stared emptily straight ahead. She was completely still. Her leg was incapable of movement. Her mind removed her from the living room and brought her to the park where she and Michael had met. She thought of the swings, and she thought of his face as a young boy and how she saw it for the first time while she was suspended in midair. She felt the breeze of the warm summer day and how it made her hair fly outward as she descended. She wanted to be there in that place, feeling that warm breeze forever. To be there would mean they still had the rest of their lives together. To be there would mean Lara could still talk to her friend, eat ice cream, and play tag. To be there would mean he was still with her, loving her.

Detective Dunham leaned forward to position himself in her view.

"Mrs. Cloughey? I'm sorry. Are you okay, ma'am?"

Lara didn't make eye contact, and she never replied.

Sean placed his hand on hers, and with tears having their way with him, he informed the detective that he would perform the identification.

CHAPTER 42

AT 4:15 P.M., FATHER SEAN CLOUGHEY STOOD OVER his brother, and, having already provided confirmation of identity, he performed the sacrament of last rites. He looked at his brother's face and body. He could see the heavily sewn incision on top of his chest, the flesh pinched taut and red. Michael's face was swollen, and, in some areas, it shifted in color from black and gray to a light maroon. One of his eyes was swollen to such an extreme that he almost couldn't distinguish the top of the eye from the cheekbone. Michael's hands were a deep shade of purple, but aside from the deep gashes from his last fight, Sean could still distinguish the small scars from fights Michael had long ago. He thought of the Peterson brothers, Dave Mantinakis, and even himself. The room was warmer than he suspected it would be, but the antiseptic smell it held was slightly overpowering. He would remember this room forever, and the smell would never leave him. He would, upon occasion, smell it in the most random of places where it was not present.

Sean looked at a rolling tray that stood nearby. It shelved one item, an Elgin wristwatch. Sean picked it up to notice the crystal was shattered and the bezel was cracked. He turned it over to read the inscription that John Sr. had engraved into it many years prior.

"They didn't steal this."

Sean informed the attendant that he was taking the watch. He didn't ask permission, and he didn't wait for a reply.

Crying, he bent down to the ear of his brother, and he whispered, "I'll take care of them Mikey. All of them." He kissed Michael's forehead and left.

Michael would be buried at St. Damascus Cemetery in a family plot that included John Sr., Virginia, and Michael's twin. Sean, many years prior, pulled some strings to have Michael's twins ashes moved into this family plot so they could all sit at the Cloughey dining room table for eternity. There was one remaining space there for Sean. It made him simultaneously feel a sense of warmth and terror. He remembered when his parents purchased the burial lot. They had decided upon it after the death of Michael's twin. They remarked that it sat on a hill and that it had a small sapling adjacent to it. His parents and Michael's twin had been gone for some time, and the sapling had grown considerably. The top had grown over the plot, offering shade on most warm days and shedding beautiful orange and reddish-brown leaves in the fall.

Lara, with Sean's quiet assistance, held a small reception at the Cloughey house. The living room, dining room, and kitchen were filled with Michael's childhood friends, former colleagues, and acquaintances. Some brave souls bore the abrasive cold to have a cigarette on the front steps. Lara was stone, and she busied herself serving, cleaning, and providing refreshments. She didn't want to share her tears with anyone. They belonged to her and Michael. She would make sure her son was okay. That was all she could offer anyone at that time. She wasn't sure if she would ever be able to offer more than that ever again. Daniel was picked up, held, and spoken to by almost everyone who attended. At one point, Michael's childhood baseball teammate Jimmy Brennan attempted to tell Daniel the story of what became monikered as "The Dave Mantinakis Game." Jimmy got to the description of the home run, and Lara silently and abruptly grabbed Daniel from his knee and placed him in Sean's arms. Those stories would not be for her son.

Hours later in the early evening and after everyone had left, Lara sat sleeping on the couch with Daniel asleep on her chest. She was still fully dressed. There were still some dirty plates and garbage in several rooms. Cups and glasses were on display on various cabinets as they marked where people had stood to converse about her husband. They were ghostly reminders. It was dark outside. Only a standing lamp dimly lit the living room. The house was cold, and it was unrecognizably quiet. It was just them. That's how it would be from that point forward.

CHAPTER 43

TEN DAYS AFTER THE BURIAL OF MICHAEL CLOUGHEY and well after the passing of the Thanksgiving holiday, four individual and somewhat nondescript packages were delivered via private messenger service. Three of the packages were large padded yellow mailing envelopes, and the fourth was a thin business envelope. The padded envelopes each held a medium-sized black vinyl ring binder. The thin business envelope contained a single piece of copy paper. The first padded envelope was delivered to Agent Angela Robinson at the Federal Bureau of Investigations. Agent Robinson was second in command of a unit that specialized in white-collar crime.

The second padded envelope was delivered to the desk of Sarah Nieves, education reporter at the *New York Times*. The third padded envelope was delivered to Detective Thomas Dunham at the 72nd Precinct. Each of the binders was filled with all the information that had been gathered by Vera Conroy, Donald Tressell, and Sean Cloughey. They were all shipped anonymously from a messenger service in Midtown Manhattan. They were all presented in a particularly meticulous and pristine fashion, and they all told the story of how St. Catherine's Preparatory was being used as a shell company for money laundering. It further went on to detail how Headmaster Ralph DiNardi, Board Chair Robert Hanover, seventeen of twenty-one board members, and Edinburgh Global were involved in financial fraud resulting in an excess of one hundred million dollars. The binders also detailed how the death of Michael Cloughey was not at all a robbery but more a direct result of his awareness of the information contained therein and an attempt to keep all of this material from seeing the light of day.

The fourth delivery of the single business envelope was delivered to the office of Mr. Robert Hanover. It was received and signed for by Ms. Anya Crawford. Anya thanked the messenger and scanned the envelope for a return address. There was none to be found. It simply held a mailing label that read, *MR. ROBERT HANOVER.*

Anya opened her desk drawer and removed a thin silver letter opener with her initials embossed on the mother-of-pearl handle. She removed the contents of the envelope and curiously opened the piece of paper, which was folded in thirds. On the paper was a single sentence presented in the same size and font as the label on the envelope. Her eyes widened, and she felt overcome by nausea. Anya leapt up from her chair, knocking over her coffee and spilling half of it on her legs and shoes. It took her two attempts to twist the doorknob and burst through the door leading into Hanover's office. Hanover's head whipped up, seeing her run toward him as Anya placed the letter on the brand-new mahogany desk that had itself just been delivered two days prior. With no words exchanged between them, Robert Hanover slid the letter to his view to read, *YOU KILLED THE WRONG BROTHER.*

ABOUT THE AUTHOR

A LIFELONG EDUCATOR, JOHN Infortunio has devoted almost thirty years to working as a literature teacher and basketball coach at Bishop Ford High School in Brooklyn before becoming Dean of Students and Director of Operations at Cristo Rey Brooklyn High School. *Destroyed by the Events of the Day* is his first novel, and he sites classical authors such as Fitzgerald and Hemingway as early inspirations. His more modern literary inspirations include authors Dennis Lehane, James McBride and Stephen King. He received his BA from St. Francis College in Brooklyn, NY and he went on to perform his graduate work at Brooklyn College. He graduated both programs with Honors and Cum Laude Awards. He currently resides in Bay Ridge Brooklyn with his family."

Made in the USA
Middletown, DE
14 January 2023

22189060R00149